P9-AOK-261

Elyse Gasco, Dennis Bock & Nadine McInnis

COMING ATTRACTIONS
97

This book was written and published with the assistance of the Canada Council, the Ontario Arts Council and others. We acknowledge the support of the Canada Council for the Arts for our publishing program.

Acknowledgements: "The Spider of Bumba" by Elyse Gasco first appeared in *Canadian Fiction Magazine*; "Elements" by Elyse Gasco was originally published in *Western Humanities Review*; and "You Have the Body" by Elyse Gasco originally appeared in *Grain*. "Stars" by Dennis Bock was first published in *Queens' Quarterly*; "Olympia" by Dennis Bock was first published in *Descant* and will also appear in this year's *Journey Prize* anthology, and "When She Flew" by Dennis Bock first appeared in *Grain*. "The Lotus-Eater" by Nadine McInnis first appeared in *New Quarterly* and "Claiming the Body" by Nadine McInnis was first published in *Canadian Forum*.

ISBN 0 7780 1074 0 (hardcover)
ISBN 0 7780 1075 9 (softcover)

Cover art by Janet Moore
Book design by Michael Macklem

Printed in Canada

PUBLISHED IN CANADA BY OBERON PRESS

Contents

Introduction

Our worry about family, about community, runs through this society like a hidden river. We prize these things, we fear them, we think they are vanishing, we think they will never leave us alone. The three writers chosen for this year's *Coming Attractions* have drawn some of their themes from this underground current of longing and anxiety. Elyse Gasco of Montreal, whose stories have won the 1996 Journey Prize and the *Prism International* Annual Fiction Competition, says that "a few years ago I...received an Explorations Grant from the Canada Council to work on a collection of stories that all dealt in some way with the theme of adoption. Ironically, at this time I became pregnant with my daughter and so with subsistence living for about 9 months I was able to work on these two fairly similar projects at once." The three stories included here are part of that collection—stories of children and grown children, adults who wish or do not wish to be mothers and fathers, to be or to stop being the children of their real and imagined mothers and fathers. "As an adopted child myself," Gasco continues, "I became overwhelmed with the identifications I was experiencing...all of a sudden I was everyone."

All of a sudden I was everyone. And Dennis Bock, of Toronto, writes of the night that he realized that writing is "both a fierce act of personal statement *and* an act of limitless generosity. Elemental, yes. But it hit me. Nothing exclusive about it. You can keep it in your family and give something to your readers at the same time. Maybe the key here is generosity." Two of the three stories included here are from *Olympia*, the history of a family which will be published by Doubleday next spring. The third, "Stars," is again about a father and a child, and a most strange, shy and heartbreaking love.

Nadine McInnis, of Ottawa, is already known as a poet and literary critic. She says of her stories, "I'm interested in moral ambiguity, what inner forces compel people to act and what these actions mean to our sense of community. The body's events—birth, sex, death, illness—challenge the sense of safety and agency in our lives.... My characters...use their analytical and meditative faculties to reach as far as they can, but ultimately find themselves on the threshold of the mysterious, the unknowable." Of her stories, "Claiming the Body," begins in family and ends in uncertainty; "The Lotus-Eater" tests the importance and the very meaning of the kind of community we call love. But the story I have chosen to end the collection, "The Human Chain," ends with a woman, in an extremity of unknowing and possible tragedy, reaching out for a vision of the human community of strangers, aware that this vision has failed before and will fail again but extending her hand. "He considers a moment, reaches out, and takes it in his own."

MAGGIE HELWIG

Contributions for *Coming Attractions* 98, published or unpublished, should be sent directly to Oberon Press at 400–350 Sparks Street, Ottawa, Ontario, K1R 7S8 before 30 November, 1997. All manuscripts should be accompanied by a stamped, self-addressed envelope.

ELYSE GASCO

The Spider of Bumba

There is a picture of you in the newspaper standing between a man and a woman that for a very short time you knew as parents. The headline reads: "Whose Baby Is This?" You are wearing checkered knickers and a jacket and a matching cap that is a little too big and droops over one eye making you squint. You look like an old English orphan and you wonder if this was deliberate. Even then, it seems you only smiled with half your mouth, always keeping the occasion close to neutral just in case. Just one side of your mouth lifting its lips in an obligatory salute. It is the small, puffy, perfect mouth of a child. Your parents seem regular. You feel sure that if you had stayed with them you would always have had plenty of fibre. They each grip your hand tightly stretching your arms up and between them in a little Y. They are wearing sporty clothes. They are trying to look fit.

Underneath this is a crazy picture of your real father. His hair is long and he wears a tight choker of beads. You know now that the beads are red but it is only a black-and-white photo, and his eyes do not look green but soot black, and his gold skin seems stone grey. He is quoted as saying: *If you suck the nipples hard and long enough, eventually even a man's body can learn to produce the necessary milk.* Things like this did not endear him to the public. In the picture he is doing everything wrong. He holds up his hand as if to block his face like a thief. A rolled cigarette burns almost to the end between his fingers. His nails are dirty and a little too long. Where could the stuff under his nails have come from? Where could he have ever gotten so messy? He does not look fit at all, but there is something about him that is almost more than natural.

This is the only fable I will ever tell you, so listen good. Your father has you by the elbow and you face him, trying not to pull away from the pressure of his fingers that seem to grind themselves between your skinny bones. He knows he is a man with a tight grip but can never remember to loosen up. And he is a man true to his word. Honourable. A promise is a promise kind of guy. This is the only fable he ever told you. There were many lessons, but nothing you could really organize your life by.

A man sits in a cement room in Bumba, a sandy town in Zaire, on the continent of Africa. He is stuck in Bumba. The next truck out of town does not leave for many days. Everywhere is too far to walk to. When he asks about the truck, the people laugh and offer him dried fish. He teaches them to use his camera. They take pictures of him sitting in the courtyard outside his room. He shares the courtyard with a chicken, a goat and many women who sit on low stones pounding manioc. They take pictures of the man squatting in the bushes. The man spends much of the hot days lying on his cot watching a spider make his way slowly down the stained wall. He takes a picture of the spider with his hand spread beside it to show how big it is. Its body is the size of the man's thick palm. For six days the man watches the spider make a slow climb down the wall, stopping for hours, waiting, sometimes reaching out one skinny leg to wave in the air, only to pull it back suddenly. The stillness, the hesitancy of the spider makes the man nervous. At night, he wakes sometimes to shine the flashlight against the wall. If the spider hasn't moved, the man has restless dreams: the truck is never coming. He is stuck in Bumba forever. On the seventh day the man sits in front of his room in the courtyard. The day is still. Suddenly the man notices the spider, crawling with purpose out his door and down the stairs, onto the red dusty earth of the courtyard. Across the yard the chicken narrows his pebble eyes and flattens his neck like an arrow. He charges across the yard screaming like the desert wind and the spider is gone—disappeared inside the shrieking body of a chicken. Just then the man hears the sound of an engine and smells the diesel, heavy like a fog in the heat of Bumba.

When you were seven, your father flattened his neck like an arrow and plucked you from the children's petting zoo. There is a newspaper picture of a small, red, plastic purse on the dusty ground surrounded by food pellets and goat droppings. It is a perfect picture. Behind the purse is a wire cage and two llamas stare out from their tangled bangs their lips slightly twisted so that their mouths seem to make little circles like back up singers saying "ooo." In the accompanying article it is clear that your adopted parents are dizzy with grief. Your mother says: I just went to get her some more pellets and...poof. Your father says: She loves the zoo. What kind of animal would do this? Of course this is the bold black headline. What else could it be. What kind of animal would do this? And the llamas with their shaggy beards sing "ooo."

What you remember about your father's car that day is very dim. The shapes of these things are seen through a squint—sometimes clearly and sometimes with great distortion. You remember a puppy named Wolf—the wiggling lure that made you follow—and a dirty blue car that smelled of warm bananas. You do not remember feeling scared and your father often reminds you that you didn't cry. This was the first time that your father called you his C.O.G.F which he tells you means "child of great fortitude." You do not understand but you are pleased by the word "great." He is not a tall man, his shoes have wedges which are deceptive, and he has an abbreviation for everything. At first you cannot imagine what he is talking about but later you learn; it is his code, the way he initiates you into his life, a language or dialect that makes you kin. All his life your father will want only to be concise, but he will always complicate. In the car your father rips his beard from his face and smiling, puts it in your lap. He says: *Look, you can cry or you can go with it. Personally, I try to be original. To go with the least obvious response.* You remember pressing the sticky hair across your lips and your father's approving laugh. *Good,* he says. *Lesson number one. We are all in disguise. W.A.A.I.D.*

It is easy to disappear. And to become someone else. In a motel bathroom your father dyes your hair a bluish black and cuts harsh bangs across your forehead. *We are family,* he says. *Flesh, blood, bone.* The words make you cringe, make you think of the dentist. It has always been that way—that the language of the family sounds so messy, sounds like drilling or extractions. The motel diner flashes a sign that says: Family Style Restaurant. You sit face to face with your father in the booth with the red plastic seats. Your new bangs feel good across your head, like a little hood. You shake your head back and forth feeling the new hair against your skin like tassels on a scarf. Your father writes your new name down on the paper placemat that says "Bienvenue." Underneath he writes his own name, the name he goes by. *This is who you are now.* He tears off the corner of the mat and you put the paper inside your pocket. Once, your parents gave you a little blue card to carry in your pocket in case you got lost. The first line of the card said: Hello. My name is _____. The second line said: I belong to_____. In thick block letters your mother printed the important information. Later, you remember your father saying: *A name doesn't mean anything if you know who you really are. "S" and "S." Sticks and stones* . In the restaurant the waitress puts her hand on your father's shoulder. This comforts you. People like him. You point to a bright photograph in the menu of a hamburger. Your father orders a B.L.T. without the B, half a grapefruit and some F.S.O.J. The waitress looks confused and this will be the first surge of protection you will feel for your father. *Fresh squeezed,* he explains. To you he says: *In this family we don't eat the animals*.

In the motel room that night—or maybe it was not that night, all the brown and orange bedspreads seem to have become one—your father explains it all for you. He reads to you from magazines and articles stapled together, badly photocopied, all their pages out of order. He is full of facts. Adopted children exhibit a lack of self-identity; dependency, fearfulness. They are underachievers. They steal. They are paranoid. They run away. He is forever concerned about your developing ego. All these things he tells you, all these things he does are for your "developing ego." These words make you feel greasy. It sounds like eggs and roadside breakfast places with holes in their upholstered plastic stools. You call it your "developing ogre" and check yourself for these monstrous changes. Later on, when you started growing hair on your body and the word developing made you squirm, your father would say with consideration: *I am only watching out for your D.O.* Really, this wasn't any better and always made you wonder if maybe just some kind of personal hygiene spray might take care of the whole mess. Your father is filled with ideas that your mother, the woman who gave birth to you, gave you bad vibes in utero. *Look how skinny you are*, he says. *It's a sign of early trauma*. Your father spends much of his time looking for your prenatal quirks. He is here to mend. If only he could remake his whole body into the perfect water dome of a womb. When he talks to you he keeps his hand on his belly.

Still, now, you cannot figure out what kind of an animal your father really was. When your life eventually settled into something you can remember, like dirt or sand sinking to the bottom of a glass, you can see your father in his dirty blue coveralls hosing down an elephant in that terrible small zoo, or sweeping the foil candy wrappers from the ancient orangutan's cage, shaking his head, muttering about freedom coming and which side are you on. His skinny fingers had the surprising grip of animals you never expect to have such hands—a raccoon, a beaver. His eyes could narrow and widen like any of the cats. But his face to you always seemed shaggy and thick, like the picture of a lone musk oxen you once saw, shaking his big head to the lonely tundra before him, taking the blows of the vicious wind without flinching. Just walking forward against it all. The kind of animal people like to call dumb.

There was never any word that you could call the other people and so for most of your life you just referred to them as that—The Other People. Your father called them the "yics," drawling it out like some country insult, but what he meant was—the young infertile couple. *Poor yics*, he would say sometimes, just talking to himself. You referred to your mother as "her" and you called your father by his first name, although not his real name, just the name you were all hiding under. What in life is fixed or determined? *It doesn't matter*, says your father one night, after closing down the lights in the reptile house, now the room just the orange glow of the cage warmers. *It doesn't matter. We know who we are. The greatest gods will not be named.* Still, in a way, you knew he was always amused by names. The places you stopped to live for a month or two as he carried you across the country seemed to be chosen in a fit of whimsy, a lightness that could only be achieved with your father behind the wheel of his nondescript car and you in the passenger seat getting older every day, because as soon as the car door opened, other people came in with the air and the lying began. The last few minutes in the parked car, when other families, other people, might be collecting their things, scooping up garbage from behind the seats, putting on lipstick or sun block or reminding each other to behave, these were the moments you spent getting your stories right. At least in the beginning, the first thousand miles or so, because after that it seemed there was a rhythm between you, an improvisational jumpiness that made it possible for you to follow each other anywhere, like jazzy horn players, or prisoners dancing for their lives.

Once, you remember driving through Hope without stopping. Instead you stopped in a town one mile past Hope called 1 Mile Past Hope. In the 1 Mile Past Hope Motel you watch a television program about missing children. Suddenly there were, The Other People, crying to the greedy camera: *We will never give up. We will find you no matter what it takes.* The woman wears the soft moss coloured blouse you used to wear as a dress when you played "the lady." Her lipstick is Plump Orange and tastes like candlewax. You are surprised by her short hair. It seems in your memory her hair hung down her back, the colour of lions. It seems that you have confused her with the Snow Fairy at the shopping-mall. Somewhere, there is a picture of you on the Snow Fairy's lap. She wears a yellow gauze dress and a shiny tiara. Your small hand wraps around her own and together you share her gold tin-foil wand. After that, for a long time, you only wanted to wear yellow. Somehow this became the other mother the Other People would sometimes talk about. How to keep it all together? You do not tell your father of this memory. He is always saying: *No more fantasies. No more wondering.* And hitting his chest so that his voice rattles for a moment he says: *T.I.I.B.* He waits a moment to see if you will get it and when you don't he translates quickly: *This is it, babe.*

You find your father in the drugstore buying miniature toothbrushes and hair dye. The Blackest Black, the carton reads, For the Dangerous You. *Look,* says your father. *The black sheep of the family is the dangerous ewe.* You pull him toward you by his leather lapel. *We have to go* , you say simply. *They're coming for me.* Your father does not doubt you. He grabs a handful of nutty granola chocolate bars and pays a lazy teenager who can watch television and punch the cash at the same time. Your father drives all through the night under one moon, everyone under one moon, and just before dawn you both fall asleep at the side of the road just outside a national park, beside the vans and wagons of other vacationing families who are probably huddled close together inside the deep green centre of the forest, listening for bears and other sudden dangers. It is only waking up sticky and hot, your cheek branded by the car upholstery, that you think that maybe it wasn't them on TV at all. Maybe now, no-one is coming for you.

In your dreams the Other People are always weeping or feeding each other food pellets from their hands. Sometimes someone puts arms around you and you can smell perfume or sweet tobacco. In your dreams they call out a name that you do not recognize and you wonder who they are looking for because there you are standing right in front of them but they cannot see you. One morning you wake yourself up singing "How much is that doggie in the window?" You are not lost or missing. You know where you are almost all the time. You keep the map on your lap when you drive with your father and you call out the exits. In your dreams, the Other People still stand frozen at the zoo, their hands held out to the animals, waiting. Something has been done to them and no-one has any answers. To know is everything. You think at the very least that someone should tell them that you are alive. At every stop, in every motel room you leave a note tucked inside the pages of the black bible in the bedside drawer: I am not dead. I want to stay with my father. Your father is not a believer. In the motel rooms he uses the bible as a coaster for his soda or a small step to reach the air-conditioner. Though one time, after too many stale candy bars from the vending machine, he says to you: *The difference between a mother and a father is that one of those words with a capital letter means God, and the other doesn't.*

You spend your first year with your father running. After

that you settle finally in the place with the awful zoo, but that first year is mostly highway dust and gas stations and when you remember your father then your memories are all in profile. The contour of his nose, his ruddy right cheek, his long fingers fiddling with the radio or just resting on his knee, sometimes absently massaging his own thigh or the back of his neck. His past is sketchy, loose and chalky like charcoal drawings. But he is fixed and persistent about fatherhood. *I am not some one-night stand. I want you to know that.* You remember this moment with tenderness. He does not abbreviate, still, in your head you repeat: *one-night stand—O.N.S.* Now, when you think about it, it seems you should have told your father that you would never ever take advantage of him, that you were not that kind of girl. At the time, it was just one thing out of many that your father told you, and you filed everything away perfectly, preparing for that day when suddenly everything would change again and someone would be gone or lost, away or missing, left behind or far ahead of you. *I was always in it for the long haul. Always.* And there it is, that dark extended hallway with so many doors leading so may places and awful ancestral pictures hung along the walls, their eyes shifting back and forth. Sometimes your father turns off the radio and sings. *Getting to know you, getting to know all about you....* He has a serious country-jazz twang. He knows how to make his voice vibrate just right, and like everything else, he takes music very seriously. He is the only person you have ever seen look thoughtful while listening to disco. When he says *"night life,"* it sounds almost mysterious. Sometimes you join him in the duet, *getting to know you....* Much later you will realize how important the knowing was to him, the facts, all the information. That what was kept from him in the best interests of everyone made his life an impossible dark space that he dedicated to flooding with light, no matter what. You have an image of your father driving into a flat movie set of a pink dawn saying: *You and me kid, we'll never be left in the dark again.* You have no idea what your father dreamed about at night.

You must master your reality, your father says, and one day drives you out to the cemetery in the next town, the one with the arched stone entrance and the greenish fountain dirty with rain water and soaked leaves. He points to a gravestone crushed between many others and tilted slightly forward and says: *This is your mother. She shot herself.* You cannot imagine your expression. From your father you learned how to keep your lips flat and to stop a quivering chin by turning your eyes inward and imagining a long dark tunnel into yourself. It was not that you were ever forbidden to cry, only that one day your father called you his partner in crime, said it in such a way that made you never want to let him down. The late movies in the motel rooms were always about young girls running away with men that looked like your father, or Bonnie and Clyde types where two people only seem to have each other against the world. But something must have happened to your face that day, a twitch, a bitten lip, that made your father bend to you in his wide blue jeans and brown Wallabies and hold you tight in his arms while you hung your head over his shoulder and stared down through the earth to the bones and dust of your mother. Your father says: *Your mother was a killer, an astronaut, a shepherd, a donut maker, a secretary, a revolutionary, a user, a nun, an innocent. She was the life of the party. She was my one true love.* For the first time your father didn't care about the truth. He would have given you anything in that moment. *I told her I was coming back. She wanted time to find herself,* he says, finally, and her lost family huddles beside her lopsided headstone and she is still nowhere to be found and right beneath their feet. Sometimes, to comfort yourself at night, you choose not to believe him. It is your only secret.

19

Most of the pictures you have of your father are black-and-white newspaper shots. He does not photograph well. It is as if the camera can only capture his energy, leaving his face blurry and distorted or somehow warped and crooked. Your father could not believe in photography. *A picture misinterprets everything. Moments should be free, not captured.* Your father believed in everything wild and yet here was the world accusing him of kidnapping, of seizing by force, of holding captive. Some people call it snatching, a horrible word that sounds like an invasion or a pornographic movie. To your father it was always self-evident that he could not take what he never gave up in the first place. In the photograph he wears a tie-dyed T-shirt that says: I Am Responsible. The newspapers call him a hippie, a drifter. *I am not some artificial inseminator*, your father tells a journalist. *I am the real thing. I am the father. The meaning of the "F" word.*

You spend most of your time with your father at the zoo. When you are not helping him clean or hose down the animals you and your father lean your foreheads up against the cages and he teaches you everything he knows about the animal. In some other place he studied wildlife biology. In some other time he was going to do something great for the animals. Here, he keeps his head down and sweeps and tries hard not to talk smart. It is the only place your father is truly quiet. You can tell that some people feel bad for you. From the outside your life looks very small. The zoo lets you wear blue coveralls and a cap that says—Don't Feed The Staff. In the summertime when the place actually has enough visitors to warrant turning on the cotton candy machine, you put on big rubber boots and spend the afternoons throwing pieces of fish to the sea lions. Sometimes when you walk across the grounds from the reptile farm to the African jungle you hear the visitors mumbling: This is the worst zoo I've ever seen. And it is true. Over half the cages are empty, but there are signs still misleadingly placed across the bars: "This animal bites" or "Dangerous carnivore," and bits of other animal's droppings, dogs, goats, dried elephant patties, to make the cage look lived in. Sometimes someone, a mother or father, stops you to ask if there is actually an animal in there. *Oh, yes,* you answer in your most official voice, and the lies come easily now. *The animal is painfully shy. The animal is in mourning. The animal is feeding. The animal is playing hide and seek. Oh, can't you see it? There's its snout.* You are amazed at how long people will stand at an empty cage, hope keeping them there like hunters, quieting each other with expectant shhs, waiting. When you see children lost, crying and turning in circles, cotton candy hanging from their sticky little hands, you do not know what to do. Most of the time you walk away.

When you are at school you are quiet and reserved. You do not have any friends but it is not because anyone is cruel to you, only that you cannot bring yourself to belong to anybody else. When you walk home from school down the quiet tree lined streets, or out on the narrow old highway that leads out to the zoo, you imagine that you are the only person left on earth, the last of your kind, wild and unprotected. It seems impossible to you that at one time you were afraid of the dark. When was that? You can remember clinging to the Other People from nightmares. All your life you knew someone was coming for you. Now, you imagine that no-one needs you. No-one thinks of you and is hopeful or despaired. You are not the reason for anything. If you went extinct now, no-one would care. At one time you did not know what you were going to be, only growing there in the dark of some now dusty womb, and yet already yourself, already packaged and ready to go. You lose yourself the minute you are born. The world calls dibs. At the zoo, your father makes a stuffed mother for the orphan howler monkeys. They hang on to its upholstered body and try to feed it fruit mash. You have never seen anything sadder. Each time your father passes the cage he shakes his head and mutters: *Motherhood*. It is part envy and part disgust.

Years pass with your father, each one more amazing to believe—is it really that easy to disappear?—and in this time you only see your father kiss another woman once. She is the "human interest" woman from the local newspaper and she is doing a story on the tragedy of the zoo. Pages of her newspaper line the wild rabbit hutches in your backyard. The dog finds the babies in the stretches of field behind your house or people bring them to you, uprooted by their weed whacker or other mechanical lawn work, their mothers gone, road accidents or owl kills. You try to keep their bare worm-coloured bodies warm and you and your father take turns feeding them from droppers. The ones that live are released. Mostly, you bury the fetal bodies in a corner of the yard, drowned by too much milk or dead from despair in your pink scaly hands.

You hear voices in the kitchen one night, your father's voice so low you almost do not recognize it. It is the first time you have ever heard him whisper. From the dark hallway you can see your father slumped in a kitchen chair, his hand firmly wrapped around a beer bottle. The woman stands beside him, her bare thighs leaning against the old wood table. Oh, she is saying, you've been to Africa. Your father does not look up at her when he talks. Only the little light over the stove is on and the room smells like beans and burned rice. The woman lifts your father's face in her palm and you can see that he is resisting slightly by the way the folds of his skin turn up over his chin. She leans down to kiss him and her dark straight hair covers his head and shoulders in a cape. From where you are standing you can see your father's hands close around her back and the way his nails dig into the fabric of her dress. And then in a moment your fathers hands are pushing her away and he buries his head in his arms on the table, his shirt sleeves rolled up over his muscles almost to his shoulders. The woman does not know what to do. She twirls a strand of your father's hair between her fingers. You step into the kitchen and in a strange voice say: *You'd better go now*. Soon the back door slams and your father raises his head. You stand beside him and sip his beer. He says something in Latin and translates for you. Post coitum animal triste est. After intercourse the animal is sad. It is the first thing your father ever taught you about sex.

You cannot be surprised. Really, it seems you should be filled with panic and dread in such a fidgety world, where all the events in your life seemed so unpredictable. And yet, even now, there is very little that can make you jump. You expect that in this life anything can happen and that all your best plans are just a more muzzled and regulated way of wishing. Your father's words: *Don't be too attached to any place. Don't be too attached to your hope*. And more importantly: *Wipe that kidnapped look off your face*. Later on, doctors will try to coax you. They will ask you if you feel powerless. They will ask you if you feel frightened. Maybe there should have been more conflict, deep troubled nights, awful anxious clashes, but you cannot seem to come up with very many no matter how hard you are probed. When you think of your father you mostly think of long nights, years that seemed like a vigil or a wake, where you sat up with the body, kept your eyes wide and aware, just to keep his strange, betrayed soul company.

So seven years later you are not at all surprised when two men appear at your front door and flashing badges with a flick of their thick wrists, insist that they have found you. They ask you your name. They show you a picture of the Other People and ask you if you recognize them. It is an old shot. You are standing beside them on the beach in front of a fried clam stand. You are clowning and wear the sand pail on your head like a little soldier. It is strange, but in the picture you recognize everyone but the child. It is an odd picture to have chosen for such an occasion. What could anyone have been thinking of except perhaps to remind you that before all this, really, your life was a gag, a perky vaudeville. They ask you if you know where your father is. It is difficult to know from all their questions who is really lost. The light outside is strange. Not quite dark enough to turn on the orange porch lamp but not quite light enough to see clearly what is happening. And deceit is everywhere. Scientifically speaking the sky is everything but this odd fire-blue but it is named exactly for what it isn't. Your father is a wanted man, says one of the detectives, and pours a package of Chiclets into his mouth. What does it mean to be wanted? Your father has explained himself to you many times. *It is important for you to know that you were wanted, that you were never abandoned, that I never surrendered you to anyone.* Desires are strange. It is difficult to know precisely what the desires of these men on your porch are. We want you to come with us, says the one with all the gum in his mouth. You will be safe. And there is your father in his dirty blue overalls walking up the sidewalk, getting closer to your walkway, and he sees you leaning against the door, the men big like columns beside you, and for a moment you think maybe he is going to run, but he does not slow his pace and walks steady and sure right to the waiting men. How easy it is to switch from wanted to wanting. The detectives close their bodies in front of you like sliding doors. He has the right to remain silent but on his way to the dull undercover car he says to you over his shoulder: *S.O.B.* You nod to him, you like him defiant, but he is not saying what you think he is saying and it has been such a long time since you have misunderstood him. *Spider of Bumba*, he says and turns away. And in the awful slump of your father's body you see for just a moment his surrender. They put you in another car and for a while the cars drive side by side and you are watching your father's profile again, and the curl of

24

hair that has fallen in front of his eye that he cannot lift a
hand to move, and for just a moment this is nothing at all,
nothing has happened, you are simply on the road again
between towns.

This is what your father says at his trial:
*The double-wattled cassowaries are New Guinea's largest
land animal. Males in this species incubate eggs and raise chicks
with no help from females, thank you very much.* There are
many things your father could say that might impress the
jury but this is not one of them. You watch your father in
the court room and you wonder: Well, what kind of animal
is he now? He has the look of an orangutan in his rust-
coloured jacket and his long arms that dangle over the
stand. He looks caught and a little bored and the whole
room stares at him as if waiting for him to do something
intelligent. One time he was a free man in Africa. He had
days to wait for broken down buses and the strength to
push a jeep from the muddy unpaved roads. He was a
game-park warden, his skin was always burned gold, he'd
seen a rhino give birth. Women fell in love with him.
Tourists took his picture, one foot up on the thick jeep tire,
the muscles in his thighs perfect. While you were being
born, he camped inside the park under a mosquito net, and
listened to the breathing of lions. Nobody told him. How
was he supposed to know? The lawyer tilts back on his
shiny heels and asks your father just what exactly it is that
he does. Your father rises to his feet and sways from side to
side. The room jumps a little. He really is an animal. *I'll tell
you what I don't do*, your father bellows. *I don't exist to serve
the infertile. I am a father.* Really, he is beating his chest.
Why doesn't that mean anything to anyone?

When they finally put you on the stand the lawyers are
all very curious to know if your father ever brought any
other young girls home with him. They ask you more than
once if you are sure. They take blood from you and your

father to prove his paternity. In the hubbub of the clinic and the general giddiness of the people around you, for one moment when the needle is piercing its way into your skin, you imagine that you are getting married. The thing about your life now is that things are inconclusive or inadmissible. There is no hard evidence for his paternity and cryptic letters from your mother are considered vague and inessential: *Come home. Come home. There is something you should know. This free love is something we cannot afford.* Everything comes down to evidence—the grounds for knowing and believing in something. But you are not enough proof, just something found at the scene of the crime, bagged and dusted for prints. What do you mean? It is important to act in the best interest of the child. This is the mantra, the paradox. Someone will first have to define act. It is difficult to assess who exactly is impersonating the child. The lawyers stamp their polished shoes and twirl about in their long black robes. Your father cries and spits and runs his hands through his electric hair making a shaggy halo around his head. The judge slams his little hammer up and down and tells your father to control himself. He confesses to your father with manly confidence but in a passive voice filled with self-restraint: I am a father too. In a terrible but predictable split second, your father grabs the judge by the silly white bow around his neck and shakes him back and forth. *Oh ya*, he says, his wild ape body shivering. *Where's your fucking evidence, you f.a.b.?* Fascist asshole, you translate to yourself as they take your father away in handcuffs. You cannot imagine it, but you are laughing. Everything about him is inconceivable. And even if he is not who he says he is, whose family is irrefutable? Who does not need some proof, some corroboration?

The neediness of adults makes you dizzy. The first time you see the Other People again it seems to you that they are melting. Their faces seem too wet, their features thawed

into a kind of watery mess. They struggle to find one expression that will not leak into another. It cannot be that
you are crying. Only they are blurry, cracking and unfreez-
ing with every minute. The man bends down on his knees
to see you but he does not realize how tall you are now and
he has bent too low. He crouches and his eyes are level with
your chest. He stares at the pocket of your shirt for a moment and lifts himself up again. He seems frustrated with
the height of everything for now he is too tall and so he
bends a little at the knee, shifting his feet as if he were
ready to spring. He seems to want to look you in the eyes.
There is nothing to say. It is like meeting babysitters again
after years have passed. Remember me? I babysat for you
once. You set my sweater on fire. Remember?

The woman is beginning to come alive. Her mouth is
moving and you see that her lipstick is not the fruit colour
you remember. It is pinker. The colour of a slap. And her
scent is different, more herbal and you are surprised that
she ever did something as extraordinary and regular this
whole time as choosing a new perfume. Later, you will learn
that during this time she has somehow managed to have a
daughter of her own which only confirms your suspicion
that family is a tricky and shifty thing. In a small room at
the courthouse, with muddy green carpets and vending
machines that all flashed "Out of Order," the woman puts
her arms around you and inhales deeply, her nose stuffed
into the tangle of your hair. She is trying to find a familiar
scent, the powdery smell of fine child's hair, the candied
smell of your breath, cheeks that smell of sun and arrow-
root. But you are much oilier now and smell of the cheap
drugstore perfume you borrowed from the social worker.
We missed you, says the woman. As if you were a fumbled
ball, a failed shot, a game that went to the other team for a
while. You are such a different you, it is hard to know exactly who they mean. What is sure and fixed? After so
much time, does anyone actually know who they are talking

to, aren't we all strangers every time we meet. Your social worker leads you out of the courthouse, down the wide great stairs that make you feel righteous and innocent each time you pass this way. Cameras and news people follow you. You feel the pressure of your social worker's hand between your shoulder-blades, your wing bones you used to call them. She is a "reunion specialist." She tells you when to say hello and when to say goodbye.

You have a box of your father's belongings, though the more you examine the things the more you think that maybe they are just his longings and have nothing at all to do with property. Mostly what you find are zoology textbooks and old National Geographics and then stacks of odd papers and books on childhood and adoption. Inside these books he has underlined and circled and written in the margins and sometimes straight across the page in various colour pens. There are matches with the names of towns you passed through and a box of red hair dye that neither of you had to use. Inside a brown envelope with a crayoned X across it is a photograph of your mother. She is leaning against a tree, her head tilted to one side so that her long thin hair falls across one eye, and she is smiling that half smile with just one side of her face that is strangely familiar. When you look at this picture you lift your mouth into that same sly and uncommitted gesture and you can almost feel the rough uneven tree bark against your back. She has one hand resting against her jeans and she has tied a red bandanna around one of her legs. The other hand she holds up in a lazy peace signal. There is another photograph of a woman who is not your mother, a blonde in Africa surrounded by village children. She wears a silly pair of khaki shorts that are too big for her and a matching shirt tied at the waist. And finally, a note in looser woman's script, loopy, curled and exaggerated, so that every letter looks a little like a treble clef. You assume it is from your mother, and though you have never heard her voice, she is like a tone in your mind, a pitch or timbre that you can distinguish from all other things that are not hers. It says:

In this world, the great charade is that everyone goes around pretending as if nothing has happened.
Well, I have happened to you. And now you know.

After, you can never bring yourself to fake anything. It is as if you are allergic and great red patches appear across your cheeks and forehead, like tribal war paint or mysterious ghost slaps. You notice that people are afraid to ask you questions. Even in sex, where the patches do not matter, where they could be misconstrued as passion, you are blunt and unforgiving. In the house where you live with your foster parents they do not make believe that you are their own. They do not try to win you over or make you call them anything special and you treat them just like colleagues, though what any of your jobs are is unclear. You sit around the kitchen table chatting as if it was a photocopy machine. Their young son calls them your "frosty parents" and in the winter you help him build sloppy snowmen with vegetable bland faces, and males and females are distinguished only by the size of their icicle nipples. He is short and ugly and wears a black patch over one eye because of some kind of strange vision problem and even now a letter will find its way to you postmarked something Nova Scotia where he works with troubled juveniles, young offenders who have committed violent acts, like poking out their parents eyes or setting their relatives on fire. You try to live a normal life. You sit in your room and study biology. You are way ahead of your class. While they examine and dissect the fetal pig you feel ready for much bigger things, a human maybe. You read about cell division and think of your father.

Your father writes you strange letters from prison. He

tells you that he has put your picture up on his cell wall. Even now he lets you in, he lets you know that you are permeable in his life. You cannot imagine what picture it could be. You never took any photographs, you never organized your memories. Probably it is some newspaper clipping, a photo where you didn't play the coy witness, where you didn't try to hide your face, but stared straight into the wide lens without blinking. *Dear daughter, How goes your post-snatching adjustment?* He is a model prisoner and he is studying zoology. Eventually he wants to do research into the morality of captive breeding and he is amused by the perspective his predicament gives him. He writes: *One day there will be a frozen zoo where the genetic material of rare and endangered animals will be kept. And in a time of crisis they could be used to regenerate a lost population, precious rare species raised by common animals. Nothing will ever go extinct. Imagine. I will see you soon. Is it cold where you are?* Over time you will come to believe that everyone's past is a kind of catastrophic ice age. No-one is ever born at the right time or to the right people.

For now, you work at a centre to rehabilitate wild animals. You know how to hold a loon and a Canada goose. You put soft elastic bands around their beaks to keep them from poking you. A veterinarian comes to fix their wings and you sleep with him. He tells you that you have the face of a runaway or a liar. He thinks your straightforwardness is an act and he is always saying: I don't believe you. All the people you sleep with seem to hate their parents and this is what they like to talk about afterwards. You lie beside them and think very bold and insightful things. How neat it is for you, how perfectly orderly, that your mother is packaged in a box underground and your father is trapped in a clean square cage. And all the others, dismissed like servants, or rather, filed away in a most precise system under the tag of "helpful hints"—like tying your shoelace, printing your name, or how to say hello to strangers, and how to live with other people, share their glasses and other stuff, and avoid the backwash of their ruined love.

On the day your father finally gets out of prison you will take him to your apartment where you imagine you will be able to feed him and act grown up. But he will be restless. He will throw all the pillows off the couch like an old dog trying to get comfortable. He will flip through the television stations. Finally, he will go out for a walk and he will stay out all *night*. You will be taller than him now and the first thing he will say to you is: *You look like your mother.* Or maybe not. Maybe you will pick him up in front of the prison gates in a run down Volkswagen, your hair long and wild and dyed an outrageous blond. You will give him a pair of secondhand faded Levis and a freshly washed jean shirt and he will change in the cramped back seat of the car while you watch him, his prison-pumped chest, in the rear-view mirror. This time you'll do all the driving. People at the motels will mistake you for a couple. Or maybe you will disappear and he will find only an empty apartment and the box of his things. Maybe you will leave a picture of yourself on the bathroom mirror. Will he try to find you again? Maybe this time you will not give yourself up so easily. You will play the hard-to-get daughter. You will flirt with the idea of family but you will never really follow through. Certainly you must take precautions. Somewhere you learned that family is what happens to you if you don't use protection. What you mean is: there are so many sad grown ups— how will you care for them all?

Elements

Love set you going like a fat gold watch
The midwife slapped your footsoles and your bald cry
Took its place among the elements
—Sylvia Plath, "Morning Song"

First of all, we are not taught to grieve. It is all improv and ad lib, lines coming in where they shouldn't and scenes changing suddenly because no-one knows how to play it. Hugging at the cemetery—we only press against each other to hear another heartbeat. You prepare for your mother's death all your life, still it takes you by surprise, it takes you by force, like the savage troubadour of your fantasies. The sky does nothing special. It just hangs there coolly, like a rubbernecking voyeur. It is not yet summer, still the trees are just too lush and full of themselves. You turn back to your life, a little more forgetful and say: Now, where was I?

Understand that it is only your imagination, something about grief and sorrow, and the way the earth smelled when you watered the spider plant, that makes her turn up at your back door and announce after all these years that she is your mother. She says: Finally, after all these years, I am your mother. Eye her suspiciously and think that structurally there is something the matter with her declaration, an insincerity in the grammar that makes you mistrust her. Of course, she is the ghost of the one who gave you away so many years ago and she mills around on your wooden porch like some Shakespearean messenger or lowly spear carrier waiting for some kind of reaction. Notice that she is dressed in shades of umbers and ochres. She has the musky aura of a traveller or a poet. She fidgets with a tassel of her scarf, something with zebras or jujubes, and you stare over her head at your garden that all of a sudden seems to be dying. Mumble, nothing is perking, and invite her in. Offer her coffee or popcorn—something that takes time, that needs to be made with a machine. While you are melting the butter over a low flame, feeling like an alchemist, looking for original matter, looking for what was originally the matter, you hear many voices. The television is playing and someone is telling the talk-show audience that a healthy fantasy life can lead to multiple orgasms. She stands in your kitchen eating buttered popcorn, a line of grease below her lips makes her seem shiny and plastic. She picks a kernel from her tooth and says: I don't know what to ask you? Watch as she picks up a sponge and starts to wipe the top of your fridge, examining the dust on every stroke. Say: Ask me if I've had a good life? She stops her cleaning, already now bent down into the corners of the stove, and on her hands and knees asks: Have you had a good life? Close your eyes and say: I don't believe you. I just don't believe you. Look down at your fingernails and notice the crescents of earth under your nails and wonder what you've been digging at.

You spend your nights solving for X. You are taking "College Algebra and Functions" and "Introduction to Chemistry" and you spend a lot of time shaking your hands in frustration. You are starting over again, a jump-started engine that really wants to go somewhere. You want to go to medical school. You want to save people. Sometimes you fantasize about starting a cult. Your new husband, the veterinarian, tutors you at night. He rolls up his sleeves and smelling like an animal, like something rich with oily fur, he says: Can't you see. You have to find the root. You wonder if this is the reason for the mud under your nails.

You can hear your daughter humming in another room like something about to explode, a firecracker or a planet. She is seven and she loves her stepfather with a fierce, tooth-bared love that makes you worry for her lovers. She is

33

watching a nature show. You know because you can hear things like: Over time it will have to change or disappear. Or: The dotty backs live peacefully under the poisonous tentacles of the sea anemone. Soon she climbs up on your desk while you are cross-multiplying and says: Mommy, your blue-green titties are sagging. You try to take her seriously. You read somewhere that it is dangerous to dismiss the observations of little girls. It could lead to loss of self-esteem or the inability to reduce fractions to their lowest common denominator. Say: Really? What should I do. She reaches out to squeeze a breast and explains logically: Put on your algae bra. Suddenly she horrifies you and on your desk begins to shimmy a wildly provocative belly dance screaming: Algae bra and fuck shins. Algae bra and fuck shins. And then she is gone, doing a clumsy Charleston out the door.

Your husband, the one who smells like a retriever, laughs at her dirty jokes and you wonder if he has enough human contact. Say: My mother was here today. She was in our kitchen. I made her popcorn. Your husband tells you that many pet owners who have recently lost their animal swear they hear the ghostly jingling of a dog collar when the doorbell rings. You want to believe in medicine. You want to believe in him, grow old, and call him Doc. You watch his surgeon hands fiddling nervously with the calculator, plusing, minusing and clearing, and you know his hands can heal you. Say: Ya, that must be it Doc. And he shows you how to write *"hell"* on the calculator with a four, a three and two ones. In the other room you can hear your daughter explaining to the cat that some algae are the simplest orgasms known to man.

In Chemistry class your professor tells you that everything is made up of atoms. He strokes his bald head and tells you that there are more atoms in your strawberry flavoured eraser than there are stars in the universe. When you raise your hand and tell him that you're not sure that you believe him, he rubs his scalp a little harder, and in a cracked, betrayed voice, asks to see you after class.

Your days fill out like forms, where questions like permanent address and local address confuse you. Sometimes you examine each leaf of the philodendron for signs of disease. Sometimes you read your husbands Veterinary Emergency Care book. You read the section on poisons while the oven self-cleans. Things surprise you. For instance, it is okay to eat an *Etch-A-Sketch* , but it is not okay to drink the *Head and Shoulders*. Usually you hum to yourself, a kind of white noise that keeps time with the refrigerator. Sometimes when you stop humming she shows up, shows up as if your life was a musical and now she had a line. She dresses like Fall, a lot of reds and oranges, sometimes brown, otherwise she seems relatively normal, the way all relatives can seem at certain moments. She tells you that she's a poet and sweeps her hands around in a way that makes you believe her. Each time she appears she seems younger to you, though you couldn't say how. She likes talk shows. She says they give her ideas. When she says ideas, her eyes roll back a little and she appears possessed or creative. While you do your algebra, adding negative numbers, she eats popcorn on the couch and watches talk shows—gory, historical exposés of women who gave themselves abortions in highway motels, with wire hangers or celery stalks. She slides her finger along the inside of the bowl and licks the salt. She says: Don't look at me. I gave you life.

Your daughter has been watching Geraldo. While you are standing in your garden, absently stroking a lupine, she appears at your hip like a cane and says: Is it true that adopted children grow up and kill their parents? You don't know what to say. You can only offer her examples. Say: I didn't—and watch how bravely she kneels in the earth to pull at a worm. You watch the angles of her golden back poking through the gauzy undershirt like little bird bones or grasshopper wings, and you know that it is like voodoo this connection, you can feel the strain on her knees as she bends, you can feel the earth drying on her finger tips—she is the only blood you've ever known—sometimes you think you can hear her veins thumping and it makes your head spin. You can see the wrinkles on her forehead arching and falling like little waves and you know she is thinking. Wonder if you should reassure her. Wonder if you should tell her that you will never give her away. Wonder if you should show her the purplish stretch marks as proof of her birth, your body's own certificate. She stands suddenly, the worm hanging over her hand in a melodramatic swoon, and you brace yourself against your own waterfall of protection, whatever it is, you think, I will go over in the barrel with her. She looks sternly at you and says: I just want you to know that no matter how badly I need the money, I will never kill you. She pockets the worm and marches resolutely into the house.

On weekends you help your husband at the clinic. Sometimes you play receptionist, answering phones, writing up bills, explaining the flea spray instructions, handing out Kleenex to weepy clients, wiping up the accidents of leaky patients. Sometimes you help hold an animal down, gripping its head in a wrestling embrace to keep it from arching back and snapping off your man's face. Your daughter roams the back of the hospital like an army nurse, whispering "hush now" and "there there" to her wounded soldiers behind the bars. She calls them her guys and lets them lick her fingers. She wants to be renamed Darwin or Noah, she hasn't decided. She is only seven and yet she talks of going to Africa and being adopted by the elephants. Because you are in the habit of taking her seriously, at these moments you flutter your eyelashes against her cheek like a frantic moth and say: But I'll miss you. Like a true evolutionist, she raises your chin in her hands and says: Over time, Mommy, you will have to change or disappear. Sometimes when you are being receptionist, the sound of your husband's voice thrills and amazes you when he opens up the consultation door and calls: Mel the Molester Flanders? Or—Frizz Catka Mulligan? This man, this same man whose voice you know can crack in a rasp of—oh god, yes—can stand in front of you and say: Send in Count Basset Hound Saltzman.

Your father calls and says: I think there's something the matter with her garden. Too many bugs with too many legs and way too much drooping. What's fabric softener for? Did you know she made the semi-finals in the girls junior basketball?

The next time she appears you are doing something with sprouts, filling and emptying pita-pockets, and some sort of nursery chant spinning through your head—how much alfalfa can a pita-pocket pocket? You thought you were making lunch but instead it has become an experiment. "College Algebra and Functions" has made you believe in the possibility of an equation, in the inevitability of a solution. It is electrical. All you have to do is plug in the formula and solve for X. The train thing no longer torments you. If a train leaves Port Hope at nine o'clock travelling at a speed of 100 kilometers and another leaves Fairland at ten-fifteen travelling at a speed of 150 kilometers per hour—at what time will the second train overtake the first? You always believed that no matter what, it all had to do with whether or not the engineer had a satisfactory marriage or whether or not he was heading toward home or away from home. You never believed that all things could be equal. What kind of world did these trains live in? Now, you are beginning to realize that some of that is irrelevant. If you want, things can be neater. There is an answer—so long as you don't question it too much.

Again she is sprawled out on the couch watching a television show called threateningly, *You can too paint!* A cowboy with a bad scar across his nose and cheek is teaching how to paint. Each week a different painting. Each week, across the country, people are creating the exact same painting. He tells you which brushes to use and which specific strokes, while the colours of the day flash across the screen. Floral Pink. Misty Grey. Burnt Sienna. He is wearing a cowboy hat and cowboy boots with thick block heels. The camera spends a lot of time examining his boots. Accidentally, across the country, confused viewers are painting his boots Soft Floral Apricot. Shooey, says the cowboy. Shooey, today we'll be painting chrysanthemums. You turn to the woman you've invented and dressed in baggy print harem pants and a white silk mock turtleneck. Say: Why is it that all you do is sit here watching this stupid television? Huh? Why is it? She doesn't look at you when she says: So I don't have to talk to you. The cowboy is saying—today we are painting beautiful mums and when you see how easy it is, you'll be wanting to paint mums all day long. You look over at the woman with the neat bangs and Afghan earrings, the one who could not take care of you and gave you away, and you wonder what it would be like to scribble across her face with Brilliant Vermilion #2. Remember, says the cowboy. Free and easy mums, that's what we want. Shooey.

You bend over your mother's grave like a branch, your fingers reaching like twigs to touch something, but there really isn't anything to touch. You have seen too many films with graveyard scenes, too much imitation grieving, a few too many still life with headstone, and you feel as if you are mimicking sorrow behind her back. There is nothing here, no stones or marble. It is still fresh, like a wound, a great gash in the earth that needs time and air to harden. Someone should explain to you how all over the world people's sutures are opening up, great gaping sadnesses that heal like skin. All your life is spent losing things—mittens, diaries, a fine designer umbrella, hair and skin—things just drop away from you, parachute away to safety. Every few months or so, your bones turn over, replacing themselves cell by cell. The shin you bruised in April is not the same shin sinking into this muddy plot. You whisper a kind of croupy lullaby—hush now—and reassure her, like a lover, that she is the only one.

Your Chemistry professor attempts a toupee and tells you that in the world there are 112 known elements. Everything is made up of these elements. Some we even share with the dead. Things like this dazzle you. There are more ways to imagine anything than there are elements. There are more various ways to die than there are elements. There are more words in the dictionary, more definitions of the good life than there are elements. We share something with everything, just in different doses, and gazillions of combinations. It is very basic but it is so neat and organized that it blows your socks off. Your socks are made up of carbon, hydrogen and oxygen.

Late at night you wake longing for a bath. Maybe you are aching to be steamed and heated. Maybe you just suddenly need to feel soggy. You can feel yourself hardening like clay and you need the drops of moisture before you can be shaped, before you can be changed. Your sleep is filled with voices. You open your eyes, saying—what? what was that? You think you can hear your mother's voice, like a radio in another room, so low you can barely make the words out but the tune seems familiar. She is not telling you anything useful anymore. If you awake gasping, images from sleep leave a residue and the sheets feel gritty. You are eating hotdogs together, steamed hotdogs all dressed with cabbage and sauerkraut, mustard, onions and relish. You are at the zoo, or the back of the clinic, stopping at the cages, gawking at ordinary pets with sutures running down their shaved bellies like so many caesareans. You tell your mother that you are afraid and she says: Oh, mustard up your courage. It sounds as if she is swearing at you. It feels more like an insult than a condiment, and you want to tell her that she has the words wrong, but she snatches away your hotdog and vanishes. Your husband finds you in the kitchen late at night making shoe-string french fries from scratch. You turn to him, holding a greasy paper towel of potatoes in your palm. Say: You just don't understand. He says: Please elucidate. And you snort a little, something close to a laugh, because you mishear him and think he said: Please hallucinate.

Your father calls. I miss her, he says. I can't find the herring. I can't find my thermal socks. What should I do with all her shoes?

Your husband, the one that knows about anal glands, believes in pheromones, and you can hear him sniffing before you feel his hands start to pet you. Let me smell you, he says—and he finds all the creases and crevices of your body, places that you wash only by accident. Lately you ask him if he thinks you're normal. He thinks you are joking. He feels your nose, tells you it's moist and suggests a diet change. When he sees your lips begin to twitter, he tells you of an old lover who used to get drunk and beg him to bury her in the front garden. He tells you the closest he ever got was playfully lobbing a mud nugget at the back of her head. No, really, you say. Really. Am I all right?

Some things are greater and less than X. This is what you are learning. You are a mature student and you do all the assignments. You are the oldest in your class, the most patient, mysteriously the most organized. You bring your own mug to class. Your daughter bought it for you and it says—*Mom. You're #1*—in bold red letters. When you sip your tea or punch neat holes in the handouts, you realize that the other students are probably imagining you having sex. You do not snort or roll your eyes at the professor. But you would like to. It seems as if you have run out of time to be gangly and bored.

She seems younger to you, less dense somehow, as if her molecules were moving further and further apart. It is an odd youngness, wispy, something you could walk through. She stands at the fridge drinking out of a milk carton. She goes through your drawers. She plays with the toothpicks, needling at her gums until they bleed. You want to tell her about your life; about your daughter's father, the one you loved once in Italy, about your mother and father, about your strange half-moon birthmark, about the time you ran for social secretary in Grade 5 and lost—but she anticipates you. She raises her hand to silence you, a toothpick poking out her two front teeth. She says: Please. Please don't bore me. She reminds you that there are many ways to lose yourself, to disappear. You want to tell her that she has it all wrong. You want to turn to her and say: No, it is you that bore me. But she is gone and you are left to play these word games by yourself. At night you have these dreams where you are either hoarding all your belongings in one tiny room, or throwing them all out onto the lawn, trying to give everything away. People come by to gather on your grass and pick at your life like birds.

Your daughter is working on a family tree. It is the kind of Grade 2 project that is supposed to encourage growth and understanding. You imagine your daughter's teacher, pale like a lamb, with a crooked nose, eating a broccoli salad and leafing through old family pictures. You imagine her thinking that her idea is sickeningly original. She is hopeful that her students will remember her fondly when they begin to car pool or divorce. You imagine your daughter's teacher taking bubble baths, perfuming the water with exotic pharmacy oils, and having occasional sex with a drama student who lives in her building. You don't mean to think these things, but really you have enough homework as it is. Who does the teacher think does most of this work anyway?

It is time to cut things out of the garden. It is the season. If you keep moving things around, transplanting them from one place to another, maybe that is the secret, maybe you can keep everything alive. The point seems to be to keep moving around. It just depends what you mean by alive. Nothing really dies, it just changes shape. When your husband, the one with dog hair on the collar, turns away from you in bed, he tells you not to worry, he tells you he is only facing you in a different direction. You cut the cabbage plant and use it as a centre piece. You cut zinnias and dahlias. You cut chrysanthemums. Thick, boisterous mums, that come inside and drop their petals everywhere. Everyday you vacuum up the petals. You know you should make a potpourri, but you are weary and the dried petals remind you of ashes. Your daughter picks the leaves off flowers. She says she wants them for her family tree. But first she has to clarify. How many fathers? How many grandfathers? How many grandmothers? How many mothers?

You never realized how poisonous nature was. You only knew ivy and oak, and that was bearable, natural, avoidable. Your husband marches through the garden announcing danger like a general preparing. Your whole garden is mined and you thought there was something gentle about the outdoors. Don't eat the bulbs of the daffodils or the tulips, the narcissus or the lilies of the valley. Beware the seeds of the lupines. Even the delphinium can kill you. You can smell the changes in the air, a thin film of coolness trapped inside the end of summer. Soon the maple will not be able to support the leaves. It will need all its water and will have to let them go. You stand in the splendour of your catastrophic garden and explain to your daughter that really you only had one mother. The other was something you were split from. Dig up the cabbage plant to illustrate. Carry the plant into the house, trailing the earth behind you like a wedding train. Tell her how you grew somewhere else, separately, an entirely different personality. Show her how you grew. Repot and look proud. Not everyone can repot with such ease. Look, you say to your daughter. Same plant, different character. And really, it does seem different to you, sitting there on top of your wooden table, a sort of strange collage of a tree.

Moments go by and you do not think of her. It is Halloween and your hands smell like pumpkin. You eat roasted pumpkin seeds with your husband—the one who can massage a heart back to life—and watch a television show about octopuses. Your daughter is counting candy on the carpet at your feet. Every now and then she calls out like a fisherman: I got two black Twizzlers and three Whatchamacallits. She is an odd costume, huddled around her loot like the neighbourhood pirate. You helped her with her costume, but now as you look at her you realize that you do not really know what she is. You tried to make her an atom, a thing you are just beginning to believe in, something swirling and so essential. She tried to make herself a zebra, a wild thing with stripes. You know that your interpretation of an atom is all wrong; you have not given her orbitals or electrons, instead you have given her gauze and mosquito netting and silver chiffon scarves. It is no longer chemistry. It is a ballet. And you understand the atoms as something wispy and evasive like spies or ghosts. She paints her face in lines of black and white and tapes pointy triangle ears to her headband. In the end, she seems to be the spirit of a zebra. And before she left the house she turned her doe eyes up to you, wide as prey, and said: Mommy, what am I? And you reassured her that she was the most essential zebra, the

43

zebra that made up everything. And just to further confuse her, because the moon was full and the air smelled like burning leaves and lost spirits, you said: Remember, everything is made up of zebras. Your husband raises his eyebrows. He is playful, he will fetch almost anything, but he does not approve of the lies the unscientific tell themselves. But you are thinking, if for no other reason than the fact that you are haunted, that in a world where people die and leave you, where you are always saying goodbye, and everyone in the end is essentially all right, is essentially resilient—this might as well be true.

The television says: When under stress, as in captivity, some octopuses will even eat their own arms, which grow back.

Your daughter is tired of sorting her treasures. Her face is smeared and runny, her black curls tinted accidentally white, and she looks strangely aged and haggard from begging for treats. She turns to you, sleepy and generous, and drops a handful of the dullest toffees in your lap. Here, she says. I hate these. You can have them all. She kisses you goodnight and her lips are sticky with lipstick and licorice, and you watch her drag her black mop-tail wearily to bed. You and your man spend the night chewing through the rejects of her pillage, picking thick masses of caramel from your teeth. You try to talk but find that you cannot keep your fingers out of your mouth. It reminds you of so many Halloweens, of so many costumes; Little Red Riding Hood, the cat, the football player, the Czar, the Bolshevik, a Sex Pistol, the baby.... So many costume changes, and your mother like a stagehand or prompter, raising the curtain, pushing you out, sewing up frayed hems, offering you her eyelashes or a girdle, anything for the sake of make-believe. These are things that you remember only after the candle has gone out in the face of the pumpkin. On the television you see the threatened octopus squirt a cloud of black ink into the water. And someone says: Some say the cloud takes on the shape of an octopus, leaving a phantom drifting in the water to confuse the predator while the real octopus makes a getaway.

Your father calls and says: Did you know how much a roast costs? Or a bell pepper? Or those Coffee Crisp things? Sometimes I imagine she's just in the bathroom. I followed her handwriting and made a soup.

You do a functions assignment and get an A. Your daughter gets a gold star on her family tree. She is very clever, she calls it her—Ances Tree. You put both of them up, side by side on the fridge—this great storehouse of food, a monument to your continuing education. Your husband, the one who smells like grooming powder, puts his arms around you and calls you both his smart girls. This is your daughter's family tree: a single twig in the centre of a piece of blue construction paper. Spreading out from the twig she has pasted cut out leaves. In the centre of the leaves are tiny head-shot photographs of the family. You are shocked to find that you are strangely thrilled with the idea that somewhere in your photo albums heads have been severed. On the leaves, in clear block handwriting it says: This is my grandpa. I love him because he lets me shave his whiskers. This is my step father. I love him because he is an animal man. You have the grandest leaf of all. It is a terrible picture of you. You recognize it as the one from the beach. Your hair is tangled with salt water and you are picking sand from your eye. You are mouthing 'no' at the camera. You follow the steady thickness of your daughter's letters. It says: This is my mother. I love her because she has a split personality. Beside this the teacher has pencilled in a frightened red question mark.

Two things happen at the clinic. Mrs. Ziggels' Shih Tzu drops dead while the groomer was tying a green ribbon in the dog's hair, and a thick white Malamute goes into cardiac arrest during surgery. Your husband slices open the thorax and massages the heart in his hand, coaxing it to pump. He opens his arms to Mrs. Ziggels and holds her while she shakes. He spends the night lying beside the Malamute. He kneels in puddles of urine and eases the animal toward morning with Valium and morphine. He watches for signs of brain damage and traces the word 'miracle' with his finger, over and over again on his knee. You bring him chicken in the basket and a variety pack of dry cereals. You play a couple of hands of Crazy Eights and then leave him to his healing. When you tell your daughter about the dogs, she starts to cry. She doesn't know yet that you can only just fill the time between heartbeats. She doesn't understand yet that a heart just suddenly gets exhausted and has to lie down. And neither do you. You tell her that there are many ways to die. Last year in your country two people died of rabies and one hundred people died when they shook the vending-machine for that dangling chocolate bar and the machine came down on top of them.

You are making a map of your garden, trying to diagram which seeds were planted where and where they will appear in spring. You have so many things buried in your garden—it is always a surprise. The ground is frozen, neighbours still have their Christmas trees up, but you are beginning to be able to plan and imagine and it makes you feel real again. You are the species with the concept of soon or later. You are the only species that can imagine the future. This is the reason you plant. You can imagine spring and a softer ground. You can imagine a day without mumbling to yourself. And a day when you don't hear the gasping in her lungs when you close your eyes.

Still, when you are cramming for finals and poisoning your family with frozen vegetable pies and left over cauliflower surprise, she sprawls across your carpet, smoking filterless cigarettes and listening to your scratchy Bob Dylan albums. She is lazy and tired all the time. She wears sunglasses in the house, little round ones tinted blue and nibbles at the cauliflower. She writes terrible poems about loneliness and Satan and children born without limbs. She stares into your closet for a long time and asks if she can borrow the pine green blouse with the Chinese collar. It is like having another daughter around. You realize suddenly that you are older than she is. You watch her grow young and that is odd and impossible. You spend your days with your hands on your hips, saying: What are you doing? Stop that. She turns to you hopelessly one day, clutching a baggy red sweater to her chest. You won't let her borrow it. She is the kind of girl who takes but does not give back—who gives but does not take back. Help me, she says—slow, like she's pulling the words from another world. I'm pregnant. It has gone impossibly far, this nonsensical haunting, this replacing, as if it was a pet, as if you could get another. You give her things. Take the red sweater, you say. You give her the Dylan albums and a baggie of carrot and celery sticks and a Japanese pear, for vitamins A, B and C. You take her out to the garden and show her where you plan on growing the Dicentras. You do not tell her that those are bleeding hearts, beautiful upside down flowers dizzy with sadness, and when she turns to ask, you bolt inside the house and slam the door. She stands in your frozen garden, contemplating the cold earth, the icy rock garden, a very sad ghost. You lean against the door. You breathe. You let go. You ignore the mournful rapping while you do your twenty-minute workout.

Second of all, there is this urge to forgive. It is why we say: I'm sorry. You suddenly have the power to forgive great injustices, crimes and let downs. This is the holiness of sorrow. It is almost nine months, and you are pushing the thing from you like a birth. The sky, though grey and heavy with snow, seems kinder. The bare trees, naked and skinny like victims, seem vulnerable. There is a stone now, a marker forever—longer than her life. You stand there, your head wrapped in a scarf, stamping your feet at the edge of her grave—forgiving the world.

Your father calls and says: I tried Thai food. I sewed a button. There was an hour when I didn't think of her. Do you think that's all right?

Sometimes when you are grating carrots or pitting cherries and you are staring out your window, you think you see her standing on your corner, in a gold and brown skirt, shifting from hip to hip, just waiting. Sometimes you think you see her sunbathing on your front lawn. She waves at you, tries to get your attention, but you are reaching for the morning newspaper and you don't look up. Sometimes you see her kneeling in your garden, weeding, trying to be someone else. Most of the time you realize who you are missing and you bake something, a pie, a crumble, something that will overpower the house. You pass your exams. Someday you might even save a life.

You Have the Body

I

You meet your man at the outdoor market. He is standing
in front of the fruits, feeling the melons and humming jazz.
He stands there like the horn of plenty—gathering apples
and plums, peaches and grapes, pressing them against his
chest, holding them there with the strength of his chin.
You pluck an apple from his neck and say: I am with
child. He stares at you, not understanding, his mouth hanging open slightly like a little gash in his face. You wait for
your words to wind their way through him, to wrap and
curl into a knot of meaning. You are patient. You have nine
months—give or take. Meanwhile, you snitch a few cherries
and shove them slyly into your mouth. Your man's arms
jerk out suddenly toward you—to embrace you or to push
you away, it is all unclear—and the fruit tumbles to the
ground. Things split apart. Seeds spill everywhere. The old
vendor claps her hands in merriment but makes you pay for
the fallen fruit anyway. At home you make a bruised fruit
salad and think up names to call the baby.
  Selfish. This is how you feel. And you carry this
selfishness around like a passport. Your borders, it seems,
are already beginning to expand. Still, the world is vast and
unsafe and feels as if it could end at any moment. Your
friends tell you that there is no greater gift than the gift of
life. They are puffy and romantic people, these friends of
yours, and remember their childhoods with a bogy dreami-
ness that makes you wonder if you were ever actually
young. Still, thinking about this gift, you wonder if a card
wouldn't be just as nice, or maybe cash. Or maybe you
should just give blood, something useful. Because once you
give this gift, there is no returning it. It does not come with
a receipt. The customer-complaints line is long. The people

at the counter are usually bitchy and harried. It is, in fact, a final sale. And what will you say when this life falls apart, when the springs and doohickeys suddenly pop right off, when the instruction manual frays and tatters, smudges and yellows. You suppose you could always tell this little life that in the end it is the thought that counts.

2

You use strange new words. You are surprised at how many times the word uterus comes up in conversation. And areola. And mother. When you say this word out loud you are surprised at how nasal you sound, as if you are joking or making fun of someone. It is at once common and then taunting and original. It seems self-explanatory, as if there is something in the sound of it that makes its relationship to everything self-evident, but for you the word has always needed a great deal of explanation. Your own mother for instance has never carried a baby to term. This seems impossible really, as you stand there patting your flat belly with your open palm, for here you are. Surely, you must belong to her; the way you sleep with your arm flung across your eyes, the way you line the crisper of your refrigerator with paper towels and keep the mushrooms in paper bags, the way you clear the plates and begin the dishes even before everyone has finished eating. All these tidy things from your immaculate mother and yet how can she help you now?

You have another mother, one probably not quite as clean, who had an advertiser's uncanny imagination and ability to conceive of the whole thing from beginning to end, but for some reason just couldn't believe in it, just couldn't quite buy the product. What can you do? These mothers haunt you. You straddle these two women somehow trying to keep your balance, a foot on each fragile back, reaching up like the top of a human pyramid. You have a sense that you are continuing something, but what it is that you are continuing is anybody's guess, like those strange games where you asked to supply the noun, or verb or adjective, but you have no idea what the story is about, until it is read aloud to you in the end, and you realize how hysterical it is to have supplied all the inappropriate words. Ladies *and Gentlemen, please buckle your heads and place your lives in the upright position.* Things like that. You want to be a part of a great generation of somethings, but it seems you are a kind of Eve, fiddling with your leafy underpants, lonely and nauseated, willing to pluck at anything for vitamins and reassurance. Really, you feel as if you are too curious for your own good, as if you are starting something up.

3

You are still flexible. You plié and bend your head in toward your abdomen. You use your bellybutton as a megaphone and shout: Are you sure you want to go through with this? Eh? Speak up, will ya. You wait for answers. You wait for signs. You think it should have a choice and you are willing to do whatever it wants. You do not feel at all like a mother; your elbows are still black and rough, you still get dirt underneath your fingernails. Instead, you feel more like a candidate. Your hands shake. You canvas your belly for votes of confidence. You wait and listen but inside all seems quiet and still. It is still too early to tell if you have a body of support.

You could almost forget. Its limbs are more like fins. The eyes are on the side of the head. Your imagination seems watery and strange. You take a lot of warm baths, your head submerged so that just your lips and nose break the surface, as if you were something feeding, and listening to the sounds of fluid, the whoosh like blood through a vein. You imagine that you are the body of the one who could not keep you. She cannot stand the smell of steaming broccoli. She eats pomegranates, her fingers stained and messy from pulling at the seeds. She sleeps with anyone who asks her, trying to fight fire with fire. Absently, she kneads at her stomach, trying to flatten herself. At other times, you are your mother, and when no-one is looking, you ease your fingers into yourself, looking for terrible blood.

Helpful people quote poetry at you. Everyone has something to say. At a dinner party with a Middle Eastern theme you fight to keep your tabouli down. Then you refuse a glass of wine and a man with hummus in his moustache recites Kahlil Gibran. You have heard this one before. *Your children are not your children / They are the sons and daughters of Life's longing for itself.* Now you say it so often it becomes like a riddle or a joke. You ask: When are your children not your children? And your man answers: When they are the sons and daughters of life's longing for itself. After a while, like all the best lessons in life, like all the finest words, if you say them too often, if you say them too fast, they begin to make no sense.

Your man is very *Che Sera*, which if mispronounced makes him sound like a Latin guerrilla-hero. He does not like to imagine the future with all its jungles and sudden landmines. You can hear him humming to himself: Whatever will be, will be. For some reason though, he has stopped shaving. His beard grows erratically across his face, lurching across his cheeks in fits and starts, leaving small patches of stubbly clear cut in odd places. You have never seen him quite so hairy and you wonder what he is trying to do. When you sleep beside him at night it feels as if he is incognito. He breathes like a spy, like someone waiting behind a door. You have never felt more alone and you cannot figure out your relationship to anything. Sometimes, when he reaches for you at night, you feel as if you are lying under an assumed name.

This is how you imagine it—when your child takes over the house and holds itself hostage in a bedroom. There you are, standing in front of a closed door, afraid to knock again. Inside all will be quiet and still and it will remind you of a different time, a time when the door was softer but just as impenetrable. Whatever is happening in there is happening without you. Every now and then you will hear a gasp and it will shoot through you like a torpedo, like a fist through your heart. And you too will gasp, like a reflex, or a game of word association. You will stand at the door whispering secret words like a game-show host. You will say: Honey? Sugar? Sweetie-pie? And the voice from the room will answer: Things made with glucose. You will laugh and feel relieved. You would throw a pie in your face for this kid. But when you knock again, a voice hits the wood of the door like spit. Go away. And you will want to ask: Where? You will want to ask directions in a world where maps are useless and imprecise. The signs for the distance between each place are all way off.

4

You are haunted by her in her new breezy body, walking somewhere, let's say, through a green park or a field of some tall prickly flowers. Her irresponsible little hips swishing, she moves with the smug jauntiness of a remorseless litter bug. There is no word for the kind of criminal she is; a crook that leaves things behind. Something messy billows behind her. "Hey," you want to shout, grouchy like a park attendant, spearing the ground, picking up garbage. "Hey, you can't just leave that there."

People tell you that now you will be complete. This makes you wonder what they thought of you before. Incomplete, obviously. An unfinished course, straddling somewhere between passing and failure. It is true that often you feel as if you are missing some essential elements, some crucial parts. "Let's face it," says a girl you have only pretended to like, your man's ex-lover, who is eccentric enough to still be his friend and is regarded as well developed. "Before this, you were pretty childish." "I was?" you ask. And for some reason you want to stick your fingers in your nose. Everyone smells. Others seem to be smugly taking bets on what kind of a mother you will be. You are drawn to these grumps. You peer over their shoulders looking for a tip, trying to figure out what the odds are. You begin to count the number of times someone says to you: "I just can't imagine you as...well anyway." Still others are even less fun. They are blunt but mysterious. They say simply: "Into this world?" Aghast, as if they knew another better place and if you waited long enough they might reveal this choice travel destination, this exclusive sunshine spot. For fun, you divide these friends of yours into two groups. Those who pronounce fertile so that it rhymes with servile. And those that say it just like turtle. You appreciate the latter. These people seem to have a sense of humor. And you have a strong affinity for this slow reptile; its horny toothless beak, and its soft, stout body enclosed within a shell.

You wake your man in the middle of the night. You say: "Quick. When are your children not your children? He is not easy to wake up. He grinds his teeth as if he is chewing something and you can tell that in the future you will be up many nights alone. He mumbles something strange and garbled. You hear: Slums and slaughters. You are losing the poem. Like you, it is growing slippery and changing shape. You lie there getting the words wrong, trying to make sense. Everything seems to be on the tip of your tongue and maybe that is why you cannot speak. You think: They are the slums and slaughters of life's lunging for your neck. They are the guns and plotters. They are the sins and robbers. They will steal your heart away.

It is not at all like having a cat. Your cat is always your cat; there aren't many changes in this relationship. You both might vary your favourite resting spots, your desires for certain foods might wax and wane, still it is all one long continuum, neither of you ever really interrupting each other, few surprises—old age, death. That kind of thing. Plus, he is neutered. This is something completely different. You could be blamed. In your dreams you are given a choice. You can be Mary Mother of God, or you can be Dr. Frankenstein. Select now.

Lying with the cat across your stomach, this is what you imagine: You will give the son a Barbie doll. You will try to introduce him to his feminine side. It will be an awkward first meeting. But hopefully soon he will develop and sprout like a proper theory. With loopholes. Because eventually you will have to let him out of the house. Like tropism, he will bend and grow toward the light of the outside, which at times can look eerily like the glow of the television set. He will come home, aim Barbie at your head and say: Pow-pow, mommy. One day you will catch him prying open the legs of the doll saying: C'mon. Show Ken what you got, hon. What will you do? You will do the best you can. You will teach him about foreplay. You will put condoms in his lunch pail, hidden between the Twinkies and the Trail Mix.

5

What can you say about your man, except that you are no longer sure that you trust him. He smells like that strange papaya shampoo. He cooks things in the kitchen, shrimps and weird sauces that he knows you can't eat, that make you gag. Sometimes when he lies in front of the television, his mouth hanging open a little, his shirt unbuttoned to his waist you think: "Oh, God. I have made a tragic mistake. I have mated badly." Shouldn't he be preening? Shouldn't he be trying to impress you; carrying sharp twigs in his mouth, swinging from the tallest tree, patting down the earth, stomping and bellowing for your protection? You have always been torn between love and solitude and you think that now you might be crowding yourself right out of your life. When he persists in asking you what you want to eat, you wonder how he ever got into your house. Just what part does he think he actually played in this whole thing? Sometimes when he sees you reach into your pants fearfully checking for drops of blood, he takes it as a sign of lust. You are so wrapped up in your biology it is difficult to understand just what it is that he is doing. Lying underneath him, your whole body groping toward some unimaginable destiny, you say: "You know, there is a vas deferens between us." But he does not understand himself enough to get it.

You are surprised when the doctor says that everything is progressing normally. You do not think that you have a history of progressing normally. In your medical file under Family History you have a lot of question marks. You do not know your disease ancestry. You do not know how your mother's labour went, except that here you are. The nurse gives you a few pamphlets to take home and read, brochures you like to call them, flashy and colourful , like something you might get at a car dealership, something you should decide upon with a test drive. Inside one of them you read: *Now you might become curious about your own mother's pregnancies and deliveries.* And you think that this is true. You might.

You imagine her alone. What did this woman know about love anyway. She wore her jeans until they bulged. She drank in dark bars and fell over into the laps of strangers. One night she went home with a piano player and she didn't even wince when he squeezed her swollen breasts. She was flippant with her proteins, fast and loose with her calcium supplements. It's a wonder you are even alive. Is it possible to fill every second of the day so that you never have a moment to think? "I seem to remember something about her being a nurse," your mother tells you. A nurse? A fluffy do-gooder student with a fat pony tail and a delicate bedpan manner—gone bad. A Cherry Aimless who failed at nursing, whose uniform pulled and gaped in disgrace, whose ankles swelled in her thick white shoes. A crazy woman in her protective mask switching around the babies in the nursery. Maybe she loved a doctor, an orderly, a patient who died. Maybe some heartless resident promised her a house in the country and then left her for a cardiologist. Your mother sends you recipes in the mail for high protein shakes and an article about soya beans. She high-lites all the important food groups and suggests fresh ginger for nausea and you realize that she has always known how to take care of you.

You go for your first ultrasound. In the hospital you find yourself staring at the nurses. Most of them wear glasses and seem withdrawn. When the technician rolls the sensor across your stomach you realize that you are watching her instead of the screen. This is a habit you picked up from watching stewardesses on airplanes, convinced that they will be the first to register signs of disaster, impending danger. Who knows what you are making in there, what strange materials you are actually made of. You wait for her facial expressions to change, but she just seems bored. She does not seem like a good caregiver. She begins to read out the parts like a merchandise list. Finally, you glance at the screen and there it is, unbelievably yawning and raising a small hand in a kind of salute. Your man grabs your hand in a sudden rush of disbelief and implication. Oh, the things that grow out of the murkiest longings. The technician asks if you have any questions. You say: "Ask if it wants to be born." Finally the woman laughs a little and says: "Everything wants to be born. It is the urge to life." "Really?" you say. Because you desperately want to believe this person who has pronounced your centre alive and well, and you have always had such a hard time summoning up your own eagerness, your own importunity. You are possessed by a strange knowledge, like realizing that most of the dust in your house is actually your own skin. Everywhere you go you leave pieces of yourself. It is an awesome responsibility. You want so badly to believe in this urge to life, but you remember high school and suddenly you feel sick and guilty.

How could you not have noticed before all the pregnant women, all the children on the street, all products of a mounting desire, however brief, however fleeting. You are like someone back from the moon, bewildered by station-wagons and family vans, by car pools and video games. What does any of that have to do with what you just saw. You and your man walk home like the first people on earth. You want to take off your shoes and go barefoot. You want to lie face down in the soil somewhere, to smell something real, to plant yourself and grow bushy and full of yourself, like human nature. How can you not feel like a kind of Eve. How can you not want to know everything.

When your child is at school you will memorize encyclopedias. You will read the Trivial Pursuit cards in the bathroom. You will keep the Book of Lists under your mattress like an erotic magazine. You will blush with useless knowledge. Secretly you will relearn how to multiply fractions. At dinner one night you might be feeling particularly confident. You will risk everything then. You will say: "go ahead. Ask me anything. I dare you." And your daughter will reach into her chest, pull out her heart and spread it across the table like a royal flush. She will murmur: "Look. Who are you? Why does it hurt?" This will all stun and frighten you and so you will tell her that the Virginian opossum has as many as seventeen teats. You will tell her that Julius Robert Oppenheimer's main aim was the peaceful use of nuclear power. You will tell her that the atmosphere not only provides us with oxygen, it also protects us from the sun's harmful radiation and the excesses of cold and heat. You will tell her that some people think aliens built Stonehenge. And you will remind her that the peculiar thing about fractions is that when you multiply them, no matter how fruitfully and with what attention, you always end up with less then you expected.

6

Your mother sends you a baby picture of yourself at three weeks, your head still a little misshapen from the inside of some other woman's body, the tremblings of her faithless muscles. You have never been all that gentle with yourself but for the first time you want to reach out and pick yourself up and stroke your splotchy forehead. You have a hard time giving away an old pair of shoes. Spiders rule your bathroom. When a plant dies you never really know what to do with its body, its dusty and crackled earthy remains. When your cat followed you home, dank and drippy with an eye infection, you cried, but you kept him. Your mother writes that you should send her pictures of yourself, of your ampleness, your unfurling bellybutton, like an exhausted braid or a pig's nose. But you are embarrassed. Not only by your plain and palpable lust, but by something even more unexpected—your natural and painless fecundity. "I am fecund," you say to your mirrored reflection, and you feel suddenly dangerous and dirty, as if somehow the very term has all the makings of a swear word. You cannot send this image of yourself to your mother, in the bulging uniform of a traitor, the grotesque adornment of a betrayer. The strange riddle twists through you with the power and intention of a snake. When are your children not your children? When is your mother not your mother?

You watch a television show about population growth. A

science fiction writer gloomily suggests that women should just stop having babies for a while, to give the earth time to heal and repair. He says you have to be careful. He says that soon there will be no more room left on the planet. He says we will all die of thirst or claustrophobia. You are so easy to blame. Your shirts do not button properly. You are slow and often dreamy. You whistle for no reason and cry unexpectedly. The TV flashes pictures of dying children, of orphans waiting to be adopted, their eyes wide and goopy with infected tears, their tiny ribs like washboards. And you think: Oh, pretty please. Just this one. There must be just a little space for this one. You cannot know what you are about to set free and unmuzzled into this world. Your very first blood. Your little Rambo.

7

Spring comes early. Birds lean up against your window like buskers, like colourful folk-singers whistling through the open screen. It is not strange to you at all that you have timed it to the month of your own birth. Life loves to be held and burped. It needs to repeat itself. How could anyone have ever thought the world was flat? It is so obviously round, circling over and over again. All the movements inside remind you of live fish held in a plastic bag, treats from the pet store, creatures you could fool yourself into thinking required the minimal amount of care. Sometimes you imagine that it cannot breathe, that you yourself are made of plastic, artificial and smothering. For both of you there is finally only one way out. You imagine the way you must have bruised her inside, or lodged a heel right under a rib, or pressed yourself hard into her bladder or a kidney, forcing her to remember you there. You waited with her like a prisoner, though it is difficult to imagine just who was holding who hostage. Clearly she must have gotten the poem wrong, misheard it somehow in a very crowded room so that she could have turned to you and said in all seriousness, in the voice of a poet: "Don't you know you are not my child?"

8

You are heavy and at times this feels only indulgent. Everyone can see what you are up to. Standing, stretching, anything erect really, is not as much fun as it used to be. All you want to do is squat. Life moves vigorously now and sometimes when you look down at yourself you can see your own shirt actually moving, fleeting jabs and undulations. When this happens in public you feel suddenly like a suspect, a shoplifter, someone whose hunger is so painfully obvious.

Lately you cannot imagine being loved. You do not know what you will ever do to deserve it. You stay up late eating cheese popcorn and watching terrible movies. Every night it seems there is something on about the invasion of aliens, rubbery things looking for a new home, lodging in people's faces or taking over their lawn-mowers. You watch these sad, awful creatures covered in phlegm or mucous as if they'd been crying way too long, battling all of life and you think: Let them be sons and daughters. Let them be songs and drifters. Let them be sinks and rafters. Just let them be. It seems you cannot stop checking the clock or flipping through the pages of your date-book. Suddenly it feels as if you have run out of time to change the world. You decide that if the one inside you needs to burrow into some part of your face or to take over a favourite appliance, you will let it. When you do finally fall asleep, this is what you dream:

One day the child will wake up with a strange glint in the eye, a tiny grimace like a smudge in the crook of the mouth. But when you lick your finger and go to wipe it off, it is indelible. The child will watch you suspiciously, the way you watch someone blowing up a balloon—waiting for the bust. The child will stalk you warily around the house, and the look will remind you of a time when people used to pick up your hand and say in amazement: "Look at this tiny wrist. I could break it like that." In the child's eyes is a strange brew of disgust and pity and you will see that this child is afraid of becoming you. All this will seem odd to you. It will not have occurred to you that you had finished becoming. The child will develop a cruel interest in your life, following you around the house like the paparazzi, asking cunning and subtle questions like: "At what point exactly do you think your life went wrong?" And: "When did you finally let go of your dreams to settle for this?" And you will know that there is no such thing as planned parenthood. All the things you will do right will be by mistake.

In the last weeks you imagine that there is another choice. You are as cranky and unpredictable as a cat. You just want to go off somewhere alone. You know it isn't his fault, but lately when you look at your man, just the sight of him makes you feel like complaining. You imagine that you would be better off on your own where nothing horrible could come out of your mouth. He cannot get his arms around you anymore and it feels as if the sheer size of you is already pushing him away. There seems to be no way to get close without really contorting. When he sleeps, peaceful and oblivious, you watch him and think: Idiotic. Nightly, you plan your escape. Two steps to the bedroom door. Twenty-one steps down the hall to the front door. You see yourself behind the wheel of your car, the windows wide open, your hair tangling into thick clumps. Suddenly, the whole world is there, waiting. What do you want? Ocean? Desert? The cold, dark mountains? The road ahead is flat and inviting. Soon, you will be skinny again. You will only wear dresses. You will never be afraid of strangers. You will drink men under the table and sleep with college freshmen.

They will read to you excitedly from their textbooks, their cheeks still raw from shaving too fast. You will take a woman lover and live in North Africa, with a turban wrapped around your head. There are many sleepless nights like these and you watch your room getting lighter like tanned skin being pulled back to reveal the pale below. You think that it is like death in the way it makes you want to tidy, to put your affairs in order. You remember all the boys you've slept with and rate them one to ten. Could this really be the last one? You rub your stomach, gently poking at the tiny heel you feel pressing just below your ribs and you wonder: Whose body are we?

9

It happens in a rage. In the beginning it did not seem quite so overwhelming, and you are overcome by shyness. A nurse, her hair pulled back into a tight braid, takes your blood pressure. She smells like rubbing alcohol and peppermint gum and you try to win her over by controlling your facial expressions. You want to show her that you will be no trouble at all. You say: "Maybe I could just do this with my underwear on?" She gives you a world-weary smile and pats your hand. Her nails are short and clean and filed square. In the end though, there is nothing demure about life. Instead you find that you have ripped the hospital gown from your body. Your man seems amused but beaten and you cannot bear for him to touch you. Later he will tell you that all you kept shouting was "out," but he could not believe that you were actually talking to him. You stare into the eyes of the nurse beside you. She seems strong and encouraging. This thing is a battle and you cannot imagine how much you must have hurt her, the scars you left. When they deliver the small blue girl onto your stomach, you are amazed that something so tiny could be so resolute, so

earnest. They lift her to you and for one moment you imagine not taking her in your arms, closing your eyes, politely
refusing her as if she was an hors d'oeuvres, a fancy canapé
you might politely decline with a simple: *No thank you. Not
tonight. Watching my weight. Oh, I couldn't possibly.* Her eyes
are a liquid steel colour and she holds your stare easily while
you trace her stringy veins with your fingertips; your powerful blood, her iron will. It seems this child will never not be
your child. What were you ever thinking? It is impossible
to be this other woman's exhausted body now, her damp
sad belly, her sticky hair, her dry bitten lips. They tag your
daughter's wrist and you will follow her forever like a wildlife biologist. You hope that someday she will learn to forgive you.

The nurse squeezes your shoulder and you see her turn to
leave. She will not turn around again, and you see that it is
the one with the braid and that it has come undone in what
seems to you like a kind of abandonment, held together by
just a plain rubber elastic. She has left the baby swaddled
beside you in the crook of your arm, your lawless hands that
would steal anything for this girl. The nurse makes a sound,
a laugh, a tired sigh, something breathy and pushes the
door open with her strong shoulder. She is leaving you alone
with this child. She does not tell you that she will be back.
Her white coat billows a little like the sail of a small boat
surprised by the wind—goodbye, goodbye. You watch her
leave and wonder: Wait. Where are you going?

DENNIS BOCK

Stars

My son is a man whose passions I cannot know. But for our shared love of the night sky, we live here together under the same roof as two strangers might, hardly talking, polite and distant as two men on a cross-town bus. In the next room he waits for twilight, leafs through a photo album of his old life—pictures of us when we were a whole family, car vacations to Key West and Victoria. I know the album by heart. He lingers over photographs of friends from university, long vanished from his life now, a trip to Europe yellow-gold with beaches and cathedrals, the apartment in Montreal with its circle of optimistic and handsome faces. After a lifetime absent of great deeds, two things I have come to believe: that a man is resistant to the possibilities of a life he has not known first hand; and there is nothing more mysterious, more profound, than the silence between a father and his son.

Over half a century ago, I gave my life over to a faith in science. I am a star-hopper and a life-long member of the International Astronomers Union. I am a deep-sky observer. For a time Matthew was a star-hopper as well. Once we held in common a passionate love of deep-sky objects. When he was a boy we skipped through the Ursa Minors and the Andromedas of the night sky, fixing the fields of view of our telescopes to deeper and yet deeper regions of space. Now he waits in the next room, gripped by a disease as mysterious to science as the farthest reaches of the galaxy.

From the kitchen table, I hear him turn another page of his photo album, then cough into a weakly clenched fist. The oven timer ticks. It has gone like this since a spring Tuesday four months ago when he first came home to me. The AZT isn't helping. We both know this. But neither of us is willing to say it. Although I know he has given in, I cradle his head at breakfast. I feed him. I am insistent that he stick to his regimen, this miracle cure we have been waiting for. He rolls his medicine over his tongue, small robins' eggs. I have a shelf full of macrobiotic diet books. Last month I completed a crash course at the local college. But Matthew wants to return to ice cream and cereal, back to the sweets of boyhood. I indulge him when his spirit sinks. Outside, the mid-August sun cracks the hard shiny backs of June bug skeletons stapled by hooked claws to the bark of the white pines bordering the garden where my son played as a child. He turns the pages of his photo album until his eyes tire and his mind wanders through caverns of memory. Occasionally he looks out the glass door, listening to the ticking clock on the oven console beside me.

I am healthy. My doctor said I will live to see 100. Aside from a deep hollow song that whistles through my left lung, I am a man blessed of a firm constitution. Long life is not something I have prepared for. It is an empty space I must occupy, a dark room I have been forced into without the light of my wife of fifty-two years, my dear Ann; without childhood friends, family. Sisters, dead.

My son is dying.

I clean up in the kitchen. I put the laundry in the machine. I plan lunch, check to see if we have what is required of the recipe. Then I sit down to my star charts. I spread them over the kitchen table, a stack of books to my right waiting to be opened. My compass, callipers, a pencil and notepaper. In the next room I hear him leafing through his photo album. I listen and wonder what I will find in these stars that I haven't already witnessed a thousand times before. What can it be that I'm looking for? What hope can I still possibly hold?

I wonder what I know of my son. His habits, his loves. When it's still light, I want to join him, sit opposite him, test him, try to understand his mood, bring him out. I want to talk with him about his life. I want to ask if he was happy once. I want to make him understand this sorrow I feel. I want to make him understand that I wish it were me in his wheelchair instead of him, that I should be the next to go.

The morning shadows shorten on the lawn, then disappear entirely. Matthew rolls himself out by the pond and watches the goldfish pick at the surface with puckered mouths. The photo album and the unmarked letters he's been getting in the mail are gathered in the pouch at the side of his chair. I rise from my seat to watch him through the pantry window. I do not move to join him. Behind me the washing-machine churns over his bedsheets. I listen. The familiar hum of domesticity soothes me, the sound of families getting on with the business of living. Everything Matthew touches comes away smelling of medicine and forced confinement. I try to return to him a smell of lemons and not hospitals. Outside, another goldfish rises to the surface to take a speck of pollen. A slight ripple meets the fish's lips and rolls over the surface of the water. I walk back through the sunroom and return to my charts.

When Matthew was a boy, I taught him how to use the stars to position himself in the world. I taught him the importance of always knowing where you are. He was the only boy in his school who knew that the Big Dipper was not simply a picture in the sky strung together prettily like a collection of Christmas lights, that within its modest cup whirled no fewer than 25 galaxies. I taught him that astronomers used Cassiopeia and Virgo and Ophiuchus as signposts to other worlds, that the constellations hinted at truths yet unfathomable to us. He knew that the night sky had been used for centuries by explorers who understood that the moon and the stars could tell us where we were and, perhaps one day, where we were going. When he turned thirteen, I took him on his first Messier Marathon. In the space of a single night, we visited most of the 110 deep-sky objects that the French comet-hunter, Charles Messier, took 22 years of his life to discover. Using nebulae and star clusters as jumping off points, we moved deeper into space, the way a tourist uses landmarks to guide himself along an uncertain road. The Messier Marathon became a custom in our house after that first year.

That March night of our first year we set up our telescopes on the flat roof of the garage. Peering, we checked off Leo Minor, Hercules, Bellatrix. Below us sat the hockey net that Matthew and his friends shot pucks into after school. All around us Oakville slept, oblivious to the treasures revealed by the night sky. Three blocks to the south, Lake Ontario surged. Matthew's mother peeked out of the door leading from our bedroom to the roof of the garage and asked if everything was all right.

"How are my two favourite men doing?"

"I'm at Ursa Minor," Matthew said. "Dad's two constellations ahead of me."

At midnight, she brought out an extra blanket and a pot of mint tea. Then she crossed her arms over her chest. Looking up at the sky, she said, "I'm no astronomer, but I know what I like." She stood quietly like that for a moment and then said goodnight.

The first letter came five weeks ago. There was no return address on the envelope. Matthew was out by the pool, his over-sized sunglasses perched on the ridge of his nose. I walked over the patio, waving the small brown envelope in my right hand. I passed it to him, then went back inside. At the kitchen table, I pretended to return to my star charts; but through the glass door I watched my son. After examining the envelope, he tapped it lightly against his knee and tore it open. He blew into the rip he'd made and retrieved a sheet of orange paper. I moved closer to the window. His head drooped as he read. When he finished, he folded the page along its crease, returned the page to the envelope and placed it in the pouch at the side of his chair.

Nights of insult let you pass
Watched by every human love.

He didn't say anything to me about the letter. Now they come at a rate of two a week, the envelope always un-marked, the anonymous smudge of the post office cluttering the stamp. The pages are always different, rainbow and solid, the bright coloured construction paper of children's classrooms. He does not want to share the contents with me. We don't talk about their mysterious origins. Twice a week my old mailman brings a new letter. On the doorstep I shrug my shoulders and shield my eyes against the sun. He passes me a small bundle, snaps the elastic band he wears on his wrist. I close the door behind me. In the hall-way, I flip through the bundle, then carry my son's letter out back, over the grass, and lay this link to the outside world in his fragile-boned hand. A shade lifts from his face. He does not look me in the eye. I know he expects me to ask, to pry like a father does. But I know he does not know where these letters are coming from. It's no handwriting he knows. From the house, I watch him through the glass door as I did that first day. He lifts out the pink sheet of paper, smoothes it against his thigh, turns it over and reads. His hands shake lightly. His eyesight is going. He holds the page against his face. In the pockets of his housecoat and the pouch at the side of his chair the colourful pages collect, a small folded library grows.

Make this night lovable,
Moon, and with eye single
Looking down from up there,
Bless me, One special
And friends everywhere.

He hides the contents of these letters as a boy protects the secrets of a lush tree fort. He does not want me to guess, to intrude into this world. This much I know of my son. Notes from a lover, a man. Who else can it be? Is this a love resurfaced after years of estrangement, a terrible quarrel, an illness? Is there hope left in those stars?

At night I turn to snooping. While my son sleeps I enter his room and search out these pages. His thick breathing accompanies me. In the darkness I step silently around his bed, bury my hand into hollow pockets, the spaces between leaves of photos. I find the letters under CDs of Palestrina and Springsteen. They are everywhere. His body continues to shrink, his sores split and multiply, his vision grows dark; but an eagerness returns, words begin to form.

Miracle of miracles, the words begin to come. At first a simple statement, a request.

I'm hungry.

I feel like eating, can you imagine that? First time in weeks.

Would you pour me some water, please?

Then, in the garden. "Dad, I feel it. I can tell the drugs are kicking in."

I stop watering and close the spout over the glistening roses. A rainbow grows around their bowed heads.

"Just a matter of time," I say. "The best minds in the world are on top of this one." I am torn between unknown happiness and terror. My son is dying. I will be the last to go. His thin face, many times older than his years, tries to smile. Only the cowlick of his youth remains. Everything else has been transformed by the sickness of the old. I am healthy beyond my years. I want to cry, grip him, shake this germ from his body. He's responding as the man he once was, as a man does when he believes he is still well ahead of death.

Later. "Dad. Were you happy?"

"Your mother and I, we understood each other. We helped each other. Hard times are normal in families." I want to sound wise, like I've thought long and hard. As I speak I see this is something a man should understand while his family is still gathered around him.

Old man, I ask, *are you satisfied with where you have taken your life?*

His head returns to his chest, his breathing quickens, his eyes close. The sores seem to open before my eyes.

Today another letter comes. Another goldfish rises. I watch Matthew's shoulders jerk. He looks to the house, finds me standing at the glass door, does not attempt to break the spell. I smile back, waving, wondering if he knows. He pulls at his cowlick, cocks his head as if listening to something, then reads again. The crack of croquet balls flies over garden greens, between tall pine windbreaks and cedar hedges.

> *I'll love you, dear, I'll love you*
> *Till China and Africa meet,*
> *And the river jumps over the mountain*
> *And the salmon sing in the street.*

Matthew's nurse comes in the afternoon. I take the car to the city to run errands. I visit the planetarium. This is my daytime journey. Downtown, I do my banking and pick up some groceries at the health food store, things I know to buy from my cooking class. It is easy work, errands I am thankful for. I need this time away. Gladly, I spend the $10 a day on parking and walk between destinations, the planetarium's dome always at the centre of my wanderings. On College, I drop quarters into the upturned hats of panhandlers. At red lights I lean against stone buildings and watch the city. I stop at Il Gatto Nero and read the papers. At Queen's Park, I feed peanuts to the grey squirrels, nose around the stationery store across the street from the Bloor Cinema.

At Druxy's, the planetarium's cafeteria, the young man I

have come to rely on leans over his book, a plain white ceramic coffee cup pushed to the far end of the table. In the summer, weekday afternoons in the cafeteria are quiet. Initially, this is what brought us both here. Like me, he is a regular drawn to this world of artificial night, this fascination with the heavens. This is how I know him. From his clothes, I believe he is a man without a home, possibly without love. He is alone. We do not share names. His youth makes it impossible for me to know him. He is not interested in my intentions. A crazy old man, he must think to himself. But for the price of a cheese Danish and coffee, he complies with my request, strange as it is. I have been visiting this place since Matthew's mother died, coming on eleven years now. Besides the stars, it is the only place I have left. Upstairs, the old door man takes my ticket with a familiar nod; they know me around here. The counter girl who fills my cup asks how life's treating me. "Can't complain," I say, shrugging my shoulders as I drop some extra change into the tips cup beside the cash.

I sit down across from the man I have come to rely on over the last five weeks, remove a sheet of blue construction paper from my breast pocket and reverse its folds between my shaking fingers. From my coat pocket I produce the book he has come to know by sight, its green and white cover, its dog ears and coffee stains. In red ink *Property of Oakville Trafalgar High School* is stamped across the edge of the pages. A streetcar transfer hangs like a tongue pressed between pursed lips. Without speaking I leave the young man to his work and join a group of children stretched out in reclining chairs in the auditorium. The lights dim and pearly jewels form against the dome over our heads. From the speakers at the edge of the screen a deep and knowing voice begins. "We are but tiny grains of sand in the scheme of the Universe. To mankind this scheme remains a mystery. This is planet Earth." A blue-and-white globe appears above us—a dozen schoolchildren, a scattering of families, an old man. Still, the answers do not come. The mystery of life. I have stared up beyond the heavens for the past 60 years and still the answers do not come. I dream the shapes of constellations, nightly cross their unimaginable distances, imagine my son's body cured by starlight.

But, deep in Mother Earth, beneath her key-cold cloak,
Where light and heat can never spoil what sun ripened

I know he has given up. My son is suffering. He cannot eat. The muscle in his body has disappeared. He's decaying before my eyes. In a final act of cruelty, his mind is the last to go. He watches his own body dissolve. The drugs I deliver to shore up his white blood-cell count also slowly poison his body. The AZT brings waves of pain, but he remains silent. He looks deeper and harder at the old photographs, rereads the letters, awaits the postman. I look up.

"This is planet Earth," the voice says from the darkness. "A blue jewel held in the blackness of space."

I take the marble stairs back to the cafeteria. The young man pushes the blue paper across the table, then places a last crescent of Danish in his mouth. He looks pleased. I hand over a few dollars from my wallet and take the page between my fingers. He chews loudly, rinses his mouth with the bottom of his cup. For a moment I am lost in the unschooled beauty of these letters, their simplicity, their anonymity. I remember my plan.

Holy this moment, wholly in the right
As, in complete obedience
To the light's laconic outcry, next
As a sheet, near as a wall,
Out there as a mountain's poise of stone,
The world is present, about,
And I know that I am here, not alone

Matthew's nurse is waiting when I arrive. Julia is Irish. Her red hair is pulled up in a bun, her eyebrows perched at a constant angle of surprise. She sits with him in the garden. I set down a bag of groceries and ask through the screen-door if everything's okay.

"All right," she says. I turn to the shopping-bag and start unloading. Secretly I fear my son enjoys her company more than mine. If there is any enjoying left. Her voice is softer than mine, her caress more soothing. She returns his hand to his lap and joins me in the kitchen. She tells me what he's eaten and that the diarrhea is bad again today. With a sad look, she hands me the list of pills he's taken. She has children of her own. I know she does not understand this silence between me and my son. I see it when she speaks, her eyes looking for something inside me. She touches my shoulder and leaves.

Lay your sleeping head, my love,
Human on my faithless arm

The summer night slowly folds into itself as the world spins its gentle revolution.

"Matthew," I say, turning off the TV. "Will you like to look at the stars? Tonight would you like to walk with me under the stars?" He's in his chair, recent letters unfolded in his lap. I feel like a suitor, a timid lover. It is years since we have journeyed together beyond the light of the garden, the shadows of this house. Not since he has come home. He raises his head and smiles. His lips part in silence.

"Can you push me?" he says.

In a moment we are out in the night, his chair rolling smoothly. As we move along the cracked sidewalk, the re-frain returns, the wisdom of our time spent watching the sky together. *"Per ardua ad astra,"* I say quietly and touch his shoulder. *Through adversity we reach the stars.* But he is silent. In the kangaroo pouch of his chair the words of a poet sing, words of love and compassion, trapped in my lungs forever. Does he know? We move like ghosts in the direction of the lake, passing neighbours I have not noticed in years, everything but their names forgotten. The MacDonalds, the Robinsons, the Careys. They sit on their verandahs and stare into the dark night, listening to my hollow, old-man steps. Single lightbulbs press against the night.

Lights are moving
On domed hills

I want to say,

Where little monks
Get up in the dark

I want to ask questions. I watch lonely street-signs rise from the darkness. I am gripped by the need to ask his forgiveness. I want to speak my regrets. I want to hear his. Dew worms blindly feel their way through blades of grass. *Blind*, I think. I have been blind to this life. What disdain must my son feel for me? He has not been drawn back to our small town by what he has here, a love for his father, or an eternal tie to this place with its tastes and spring madrigals, but because he is alone and there is nowhere else to turn. *Son*, I want to say. *Have I been a father to you?* But I am afraid he will answer with this dumb acceptance of pain. I owe this life the many regrets I have stored over time and held safely in the distant sky. An ignorance and denial of a world of passion. *I am sorry*, I want to say. *Is it possible I do not know my son at the edge of all this beauty and disaster?*

At the lake the water is still, a great reflector of the night sky. The stars shimmer at our feet, lying like flowers in an open field. I roll Matthew onto the small peer at the bottom of our street. Where the water nips at the old stone in a broad game of tide and time, we sit and stand. My tired arms hang loosely at my sides. I have rolled my son farther than before, farther than I could ever imagine. Matthew's thin hands rest in his lap. I am hoping for a rain of falling stars, for him to rise from his chair and dive into the cool water. I want to blame something for this silence. *Old fool. Old, old fool.*

"Son," I say quietly, looking out over the water. "Did you know love? Real love?" He waits a moment, his breathing slows. His head nods. Yes.

"But it wasn't a love your mother and I could understand."

"You didn't want to understand."

"Those letters? Is that what those letters are?"

"Yes," he says.

"You're loved now?" I say, my voice rising with elation. I cup his shoulder in my palm and watch the dark shore circle around us. There are no lights but that of the stars down here, the big houses asleep and dark. The sound of a stone, a pebble dragged from the land by the tide. "Do you know why he doesn't come here?"

"He's afraid. Maybe he can't. Maybe he's sick."

"What would you think if he did?"

"He shouldn't do that," he says. "It's too late for that."

I want to ask if he knows who's sending these love notes. *Who's the poet?* I want to say, but I'm not supposed to know the contents of these letters. Instead I lower myself to my son's face and say, "Would you swim now if you could, like in the old days? Will you come to the water with me?" I listen to myself speak this absurd invitation. "Will you do this with me?"

"Into the water?"

"Yes," I say. "I'll take care of you." I slide my hands under his knees and behind his back. He rises with me from his chair, my arms his cradle, as if he were a boy again. I step over the loose skipping stones that we bounced off the summer lake twenty years ago, this pond of stars, and feel the cold waters rise against my old legs. I stumble for a moment, catch myself, and continue forward. Matthew breathes against my cheek, his arms clasped around my neck. "Are we going in?" he says weakly. "I hear splashing. I feel it now." His face turns to the dark horizon and, in a breath, we are buoyant. I strain on the very tips of my toes. We move silently through wondrous skies. I believe he does not feel my hand on the back of his head as I bring him down into my chest, hugging him with the strength of a child. *Listen*, I want to say. *Listen to my old man's heart.*

Olympia

*Only what is entirely lost demands to be endlessly named; there is
a mania to call the lost thing until it returns*—Günter Grass.

Almost a year to the day after my grandmother drowned in
a boating accident, my uncle Günter came to us from Germany and found cracks at the bottom of our swimming-
pool. This was August, 1972, the summer water almost
killed me. First because there wasn't enough of it; and later
because it came close to taking me the same as it had taken
my grandmother.

Because the war stories had always been a part of my
family, I thought I knew something of my mother's brother.
I was the son of war babies. I didn't believe there were any
secrets between us. All the grown ups around me then had
lived through war, including my father, and everybody had
a story they seemed willing to share—friends of my parents,
the teller from Frankfurt who worked at the Bank of Montreal at Lakeshore and Charles and spoke to my father in
whispers over folded fives and twenties. It seemed that everyone my parents knew back then had escaped to this
country from that dark place, as they had, soon after the
war ended. But it took me until that summer to find out
that there were things I hadn't been told, that there were
secrets in my house.

My mother spent her war years in the north of Germany,
trapped there among falling bombs. She told me about
brushing her teeth with salt, the constant drought under
her tongue, how they ate nothing but salted cabbage, about
the dead man who fell from the sky and lay in the front yard
of their house through the month of May and into June,
how an old woman from the neighbourhood came by with
a bucket of salt every week and sprinkled it over the body
to keep the fumes down until the town came and took

him away.

She, my uncle and their mother—the father already half dead in the salt mines near Odessa, the mineral of dehydration sucking the liquids through his skin, his eyeballs, bringing his lungs, his hunger to the ridge of his teeth. The three of them, six months in a basement. And when the end finally came, collected onto rail cars and rolled over the great smouldering landscape to the shores of the Gulf of Riga where they were released like sickly cattle into a February blizzard. Then hopping freight cars to get back, holding her little brother's hand dry with fear as they ran, and she the hand of her mother, the three of them grasping out for the invisible hand that reached from the tousled boards of departing freight cars and missing, always missing that train, that hand, walking and waiting and running again. Four months to return home and nothing left but stories of salt and drought, stories that in my boyhood meant as much to me as television, as the map of the untravelled world.

Before Uncle Günter came that summer, I found purpose in the meaning of those stories. Even then I used them to protect myself. I needed the train story to protect me from the true meaning of *cattle car*. But the salt connection didn't occur to me until I saw Günter down there at the bottom of our bone-dry swimming-pool. I didn't understand the salt then, what the drought behind my mother's tongue meant, behind her brother's eyes. It was the trains I saw them riding up to the hanging lip of Sweden. In school we'd seen films of Jews rolling into the camps on those cattle cars, thousands of them at a time. The image of my mother and her little brother aboard one of those wagons shining in my head as brightly as they shot out from those dark spinning reels at the back of the classroom melded with stories of displacement and organized death. After history class I dreamt my mother came to me with forgiveness, sometimes offering. "Sweetheart," she said, "we all suffered.

No one person more than the next." But in my dreams and in my waking life I didn't believe her. I'd seen those films of men and women, ghosts already, waiting to die. I used my mother's story, told it to my teachers and to anyone who would listen, used it to show how my people had paid. But I knew we hadn't paid enough.

She was losing water. The summer drought had already been declared. It wasn't until early August, when my uncle and Monika came to Oakville to spend the summer with us, that we realized where the problem lay. Hairline cracks, practically invisible, were spreading like transparent veins along the walls and the bottom. Uncle Günter and his wife Monika were from Fürstendfeldbruck, a small town outside of Munich. In the letters we got before they arrived they said they planned to stay with us for six weeks, with a weekend trip here and there around the province and down into New York. They wanted to get away from Munich before the Olympic Games quadrupled the size of their town. But once Uncle Günter saw the condition our pool was in, he wanted to crawl down to the bottom and begin repairing those invisible cracks, a job, he assured my parents, that would take three, maybe four days. That's how he came to dominate our summer the way he did, to prolong our thirst.

Günter and Monika spoke German with my parents, although when Ruby and I were around—which was most of the time—Monika spoke English to us in a British accent. She sounded like Diana Rigg from *The Avengers*. She had spent the war years in England. Günter's English wasn't as good as my parents'. I'd long since been unable to hear their accent, but during open house at school and around the neighbourhood I knew it revealed them as the immigrants they were, the tellers of war stories.

Everything I saw in Günter, everything he did that summer, everything I heard him say—in German and in his broken English—I attributed to the war. The war had shaped him like it had not shaped, could never shape, my mother. He was tall, taller than my father, and had a sunken chest that looked as if it were pushing the life out of his heart and lungs. At school we called kids like him *fish eyes*. He didn't look at you so much as stare, blinking uncontrollably over those protruding, round mirrors. He was a construction worker, his large callused hands constantly moving at his sides like the sands of a shifting desert floor.

When we got home after picking them up at the airport, we walked them around the house, showed them the guestroom with the view to the street and a thin slice of Lake Ontario, her winding shoreline already receding for the dry air that had been haunting our summer. We took them into the backyard where my mother showed them her garden. Ruby and I followed behind at a safe distance, listening to their foreign voices and punching each other in the arm. My mother pulled aside the browning rhubarb leaves she'd been trying to keep alive beside the peach tree and offered up a sniff of hard Ontario soil to her brother's nose. I watched him sniff a stream of dust. His fish eyes rolled back into his head. It looked like he was going to hurt himself, but he inhaled again, even deeper. Breathing in the dust. *This* was my mother's brother? I thought. My uncle? I watched his eyes roll back around to the world, to me, and a smile pull at his mouth and cheeks. The dirt drained off between my mother's fingers. Ruby gave me a shot in the shoulder and took off around the house.

The five of us walked across the grass and looked down into the dry pit of our swimming-pool. My father was the Mister Fix-It of the family. That spring he'd repaired all the eaves on our house in one day. He considered, his hand on his chin. *"Ich habe keine Zeit fur solche Blöde Sachen,"* he said then, pointing over the dry hole and looking at his in-laws. There just wasn't time to replaster the whole pool.

When he said that Uncle Günter jumped down onto the blue cement of the shallow end, got down on his knees, and started running his hands over the walls and floor. He closed his eyes. He looked like a blind man looking for a fallen key. Then he slid on his haunches down into the deep end and did the same thing. When he climbed back up onto the deck and started talking in German, I heard my mother and father begin to say *no* again and again, no way, that much I could tell, *nein, nein, nein,* but Günter shook his head and smiled and rubbed his dry hands together. Monika stood beside me, frowning, but why I couldn't tell.

Günter was bent on fixing our pool. He'd flown here with his wife to visit his only sister and the brother-in-law he'd never met before, and their two children, and the first thing he wanted to do was to get to work plastering the walls and bottom of a dried-out hole in the ground. My parents didn't like the idea. They were mystified and uncomfortable. That's not why he'd come, they reminded him. But when they found him down there the next morning slowly sanding the chlorine film and dried algae off the walls, they couldn't coax him out.

"Okay," my mother said in English later that morning on the deck, looking down, a cup of coffee in her hand. "A day or two of this, then the vacation starts." Günter looked up and smiled.

"Maybe this is his way of getting over culture-shock," my father said on the front porch the second night after Uncle Günter and Monika had gone to bed. I was upstairs in my mother's sewing-room, my head pushed out into the night. "It'll pass. He'll snap out of it soon."

The great unknown in Munich was who would take home the most medals, how many consecutive back flips Olga Korbut could manage before she spun off into the clouds. The sound of my uncle working in the backyard drifted through the open living-room window while Ruby and I, dressed in matching track suits, watched the Games. We were both going to be Olympic gymnasts. Ruby lay on the floor, her chin cupped in both hands, studying the impossible postures of her heroes. She sat in the splits for hours at a time. I did 100 push-ups every morning and held handstands during commercials. The Canadian team was twelfth out of fifteen. I fantasized about how things would be different if I'd been born Romanian or Russian or Japanese, how I'd be competing, and winning. Anything but who I was.

Around our house that summer the great mystery was how long Günter could sit at the bottom of our pool, drinking cups of coffee prepared for him by my mother and saying *"Verflixt heiss!"* to himself as he dragged his plaster-covered sleeve across his forehead. Every afternoon when my father got home from work he found Günter in the kitchen leaning against the counter drinking coffee, the peach or gooseberry or rhubarb pie my mother had made for that evening's dessert sitting half-eaten on the table. In the next room Ruby and I dreamed of gold medals and of our first real swim of the summer. Rain threatened, but finally never came. It hadn't rained since early July. It felt like the whole town was burning up. And at five-thirty I watched a frown fall over my father's face as he walked past us on his way to the bathroom to get cleaned up before supper.

I felt the tension seep through the wall of that foreign language that first Saturday with my uncle and Monika. It was a hot and sticky evening. We ate at the picnic table under the tall pines in the backyard. I felt something when my mother and Günter spoke to each other, me on the other side, as clearly as a hand brushing over my face. But as subtly, as indistinctly as the water had drained from the shell of our pool. I imagined she was upset because her brother was denying something of her hospitality.

"Beautiful," my father said, sensing something danger-ous. I bit into my hamburger. "One of the biggest jobs we've ever done," and began to tell us about the boat he was designing at the shop, a 60-footer on order from Ber-muda. Then, for Günter's sake, he switched into German. I

chewed as he spoke, counting in my head the number of
medals the Bermudan team had won so far. Monika sat
across from me. I put down my burger, reached for the wine
bottle beside her plate, filled her glass. My mother was always reminding us to be polite. Monika pulled her long hair
behind her ear, touched my arm to say enough. Her touch
ran to the pit of my stomach like a vein of butterflies. My
uncle looked at me from the other end of the table. I
blushed. My father stopped. Neighbours on the other side
of the cedar fence were playing croquet. Someone gave the
ball a good whack.

"We got a bronze in sailing today," I said, clearing
my throat. "Soling class." Monika looked at me blankly.
"Three-man keelboat," I added, as if to reassure her. "You
guys got a bronze in the Flying Dutchman class." I looked
at Günter when I said *You guys*, and blushed again. Monika
had a beautiful face. There was a silence. She looked at me
and pulled her hair back behind her right ear again.
Women my mother's age never wore their hair below the
shoulder. My uncle sipped his wine. My mother looked at
me and smiled.

"Looks like we're neck on neck," my father said, coming
back out to English. "A bronze each."

I think my father was the first one to see how things
were going to go between my mother and uncle. When the
silence came the following evening, he quickly asked Ruby
and me to put on our own little Olympiad. Right there, in
the middle of dinner. "Okay," Ruby said happily, without
any coaxing and bounced across the parched grass before
our mother could protest, cart-wheeling and back-flipping
and spinning through the air. When she came to a stop,
panting and smiling, she threw her arms up to the sky and
thrust out her small chest. My father stood up in his seat.
"The judge in blue concedes a perfect 10." When she came
back to the table, I jumped up onto my hands, the world
turning upside down, the grass suddenly my sky, and held

the earth against my palms and fingers for as long as I could. Atlas inverted. From there I saw my uncle staring at me stone-faced.

Ruby scored higher than I did, but I knew that was because she was younger and that our mini Olympics were meant to bring us together. I knew they were meant to head off something coming between my mother and my uncle. And for a while they did. That evening after supper Monika sat in a lawn chair out on the grass with her wine glass hanging low to the ground, whistling out scores along with my parents until the August light began to fold in upon itself and the sounds of croquet balls and the splashing of distant swimming-pools grew faint and cool around the neighbourhood. When I let go of the earth for the last time that night and returned to my feet, blood resuming its equilibrium, my uncle was gone.

We began clearing away the table, everyone except Uncle Günter taking his or her share back to the kitchen. He was standing out on the front porch, alone, his hands in his pockets. I saw him there when I delivered my first load of dishes. Back out by the picnic table, I saw my father walk over the lawn and pause at the edge of the dry swimming-pool, looking down at the hard, cracking cement. I watched his face drain of all the joy that had filled him at our performance, all the pleasure that had been his, as if that empty hole in the ground were sucking up his vitality and his pride. No-one else seemed to notice his grief the first night he stood at the edge of the pool shaking his head in disbelief; no-one noticed that night how that empty pool drained the life out of him. At the time I didn't think my father's melancholy had anything to do with Uncle Günter's slow work, or the tension between my mother and my uncle. I thought it was my grandmother. How she'd drowned the year before, the day she and my grandfather had chosen to renew their vows. I guessed he was looking for her down there in some way, that these people had brought from Germany unwanted memories, unwanted stories along with their appetite for wine and reparations. I guessed he was thinking about losing his mom.

By late August Olga Korbut was wowing the whole world, and Uncle Günter was up to eight coffee breaks a day. He wanted to stay down there. Working and standing around. My mother and father wanted him out. Monika had taken to borrowing the Chrysler and disappearing every day. I guessed she'd had enough of waiting for Günter. She drove to the Elora Gorge, Niagara Falls, Detroit and Ithaca. She went to Toronto a couple of times a week, to London, Kingston and Thousand Islands. When she was gone, when an event Ruby and I didn't much care for came on TV, we went out to the backyard, hung our feet over the side and watched our uncle stand around at the bottom of the pool. On the grass we played under the sprinkler to bring home to him our desperation, our need of water. I thought the pool would remain dry forever. I walked around the house all day, drinking water from a glass. Günter had become a fixture down there, his trowel, the cement mixer my father had reluctantly borrowed from a friend from work, the three moon-eyed bubbles of the level watching his slow dance among the forgotten artifacts at the bottom of a dried sea.

One day, after playing in the sprinkler, we sat on the deck with our glasses of water and listened to Günter speak to us. Neither of us understood a word. For the whole afternoon he told us what sounded like stories. We sat there, embarrassed to stop him, forced to listen to the end of his ramblings, sipping, forever sipping. Sometimes as he spoke he became angry and then immediately fell silent, or laughed and slapped an open palm against his thigh. We sat at the edge of the hole in the ground and watched him move slowly like a lion in a pit among his tools, picking up things and examining them, holding them against the sun over our heads as he spoke, then gently returning them to where they had been. Clouds of dry cement dust rose from the bottom of the pool and mushroomed over our heads, caking our throats as we watched him cover palm-sized patches of the pool as if he were painting a white curtain over an old movie set from 20,000 *Leagues Under The Sea*.

On a Saturday night in late August, after Günter and Monika had been with us for three weeks, my parents left me in charge of Ruby. They took uncle into the city to go dancing at Club Edelweiss, a German-Canadian restaurant where my father sometimes played accordion with a band, or soloed for small parties. When Günter reluctantly agreed to go, Monika suddenly developed a headache. She said she was tired from her day of sightseeing. She sat on the front porch with Ruby, a glass of wine in her hand, and waved when the car pulled out of the driveway. I went around the back and climbed into the pool for the first time.

I jumped down into the shallow end, like Günter had that first day, and began to explore. I kept my eyes open. I wanted to go deep. I wanted to find out something about my mother's brother. I knew nothing but the war stories, the outstretched hands reaching for freight trains. In *Decisive Decades,* our school history text, I'd read about the Potsdam Conference, the great shifting of borders after the Control Council agreed to deport more than six million Germans beyond the Oder-Neisse line. I knew this was the uprooting of my mother's people. I slid down the dusty incline on my haunches and felt the sides of the pool squeeze the world into a box of evening sky above my head. At my feet extension cords twisted like snakes, trowels sharp and weapon-like, a sawhorse, the three-foot level, a half-used bag of cement and an old red toolbox.

"You don't want to be anything like him, do you?"

I looked up. The sun was setting behind the apartments across the street from the house. A last shaft of light spiralled between the buildings and lit up Monika's face at a ninety-degree angle, collecting in the glass of wine in her right hand. "What's down there for you?" she said.

"I dropped something."

"Well get it quick and get back up here or he'll rub off on you," she said, then walked away.

In the kitchen the next day, while I was getting a handful of cookies for Ruby and myself, Günter came in and said in his broken English, "I need help. Come here." I didn't answer him. He poured himself a glass of lemonade, drank it down and walked out of the kitchen. I followed him into the backyard, jumped down into the shallow end and felt the cookies in my pocket snap into little bits.

"You a smart boy?"

I nodded. "But I'm not very good with my hands."

"Hold this." He handed me a trowel. "Make so." He started smoothing cement along the north wall of the deep end. I watched him for a minute. He started whistling. Then he stopped and turned to me. *"Ja?"*

I stooped over, took some plaster onto my trowel and stepped up to the nearest wall. I hesitated. I remembered what Monika had said about him rubbing off on me. But he was my mother's brother, after all. What harm? How would you want him to treat the both of you in his country? I remembered my mother asking us in the car as we drove to the airport to pick them up.

"You watch too much TV," he said.

I was spreading the plaster in broad arcs. I stopped and turned around. "The Olympics are important," I said. "It's the Family of Nations."

"Okay," he said, "get lost."

Into the fourth week of the visit—during which not an ounce of rain had fallen from the sky—my mother told us on a Saturday morning that we were going to Kelso. We were going to find water. We were going to bathe in clean cool water.

The artificial lake is the main attraction at Kelso. There are two beaches on the south shore, divided by a grassy hill on top of which sits a parking lot and, on the opposite slope, the outfitters where my father and I had, on a couple of occasions, rented a sailboat. No matter how hard the sun comes down on you there, no matter which shore you stand on, you can always hear the traffic going by on the highway just beyond the poplar and spruce trees on the north hill. There are rainbow in the lake, too, but I'd never caught anything other than rock bass and sun fish, though I'd always wanted to catch a trout. That Saturday I brought my fishing-rod along with me just in case.

After we got organized in the parking-lot, unloaded the picnic baskets and towels and umbrella and magazines and my fishing-rod, the six of us walked down the wooden stairs to the beach like three distinct couples. Monika, her large floppy sun hat flapping like a bird, walked a step ahead of her husband. He looked sullen. He hadn't spoken in the car the whole way up. My mother seemed nervous. She swung the picnic basket about grandly from hand to hand, distracting attention from something. Was she thinking about her brother? Then I wondered if it was the memory of last summer that was bothering her, if she was worried about my father. If this trip to water would trigger the memory of his mother's drowning. But my father joked with Ruby and me as we walked down the wooden stairs. On the way here he'd worn a pair of black sunglasses. Ruby said he looked like a gangster. Half-way down the stairs he turned around to us, his rolled up towel hidden clumsily under his baggy summer shirt like a bag of money, and said in a terrible Italian accent, "Meester Capone wantsa you to doa littlea favore fora la Familia," and Ruby laughed and jumped up for his glasses like a little barking dog. I carried the rod and tackle and the second lunch basket. We'd all changed into our bathing-suits at home.

We found an empty stretch of sand at the far end of the first beach, close to an old man and woman. Someone's grandparents, I imagined. But they were alone. No kids. No grandkids. Their loose skin covered their bodies like a fluorescent wrap. My father and I smoothed out the hot sand with our bare feet. We laid out our towels side by side, six in a row like the colourful stained-glass windows of a church. We peeled off our street clothes, settled down and waited to get hot enough to go in. Ruby went down to the shore and waded in up to her knees to check the water. I sat down beside Monika.

"Have you caught fish in here?"

"Some," I said. Her legs stretched out beside me. She was wearing a bikini. Her long brown hair shone in the sun. My mother always wore a one-piece. No mothers on the beach wore bikinis. No other women had long hair. Monika had never had a baby. Her stomach was flat and her legs were still slender. She was twirling a long brown lock in her fingers, eyes closed, right knee raised slightly in the air, her breasts pulling apart from the centre of her chest in a way that made me want to keep looking. She asked me the question about the fish without opening her eyes, without looking at me. Then I saw my uncle watching me over the rim of his sunglasses. I turned away and faced the lake.

There were a lot of people swimming, splashing around on inflatable mattresses and dinghies. I walked alone along the edge of the water. I couldn't get Monika out of my head. I wondered if Günter had known what I was thinking. I watched the red and green sailboats out on the lake, their white hulls pulled up on the wind, shining against the water. They picked up speed and skimmed across the small lake, lowered because of the drought, and then, trapped, tack back against the wind. I tried thinking about sailing, about the fishing I would do later that afternoon, about gymnastics. I tried to think about the Olympics. But Monika kept coming back to me. I entered the shade of the woods and leaned my back against an elm and looked for Monika's pink skin among the crowd in the distance. I waited under an overhanging elm branch hoping, impossibly, that she'd come to me into the dark woods, that she'd join me, leave my uncle, that old blinking fish from the bottom of our swimming-pool. I waited. I put my hand down the front of my bathing-suit and remembered the sight of Monika in the lawn chair, her long legs crossed like I thought only movie stars crossed their legs, calling out scores, the glass of wine hanging low to the ground before she raised it to her red lips. I closed my eyes and saw her on the beach in her bikini, her breasts pulling away from her, one toward me, the other off on its own, its hard dark eye staring down a lucky admirer. When I finished I cleaned my hands on the grass at the base of the elm, then walked back into the sunlight. I was still trembling a little. Everybody was in the water except my uncle. My father called for me to come in when he saw me. Uncle Günter sat watching all alone up on the beach, his sunglasses pulled up over his face. I wondered if he knew what I'd just done.

After lunch I took my fishing-rod and tackle to the other end of the lake and fished the small stream that fed the reservoir. From there I could see the two beaches stretching out over the opposite shoreline, the hill rising between them like a broad nose. With my hands I dug up some worms, put them in the small plastic container I kept in my tackle box and slid the first worm along a size 14 hook. I threw it out into a pool and let the worm sink to the bottom. I caught a trout for the first time in my life. Slick and spotted. He was beautiful. I killed him with my pen-knife and dropped him into a plastic bag. He wasn't a prize, but he was big enough to keep. In an hour I caught three more pan-size rainbows. Before leaving the stream I rinsed the blood off the fish. I carried the plastic bag in my left hand as I walked back to the beach. It thumped against my thigh with every step. By the time I got back a little puddle of blood had formed in the heavier corner of the bag.

When I held it up for everyone to see, Ruby made silly noises and plugged her nose. My mother peered her eyes down over the lip of stretched plastic. I told my father what I'd used, what part of the stream I'd fished, how each fish had hit. With a finger under the gill I scooped up the biggest trout and held him up in the air. Monika leaned on an elbow. I described how I'd moved each one to the top of the pool and enticed them to jump by lifting the tip of the rod against the sky. The old couple listened to my story from the next set of beach towels. My mother emptied out what was left in the cooler, a bit more egg salad and some juice, and laid out the trout side by side. I looked at the grandparents again. The man had gone back to rubbing lotion onto his wife's shoulders, first warming the cream in his large hands. She faced the water. That's when I saw a series of numbers tattooed into his right hand, small and blurred with age against his white skin.

My mother sat in the shade of the umbrella. She was flipping through a magazine with Ruby, the one she always had lying around, *Pattern & Design,* pointing out the dresses and sweaters she wanted to make for her for the fall. Monika was still in the sun. She was working on the last of the wine from lunch. After the fish went into the ice box she'd stretched out on her back. With a twinge I saw the line of sweat in the slight crease of her abdomen.

"The wind's good, Peter," my father said. "What do you say?"

I grabbed my shirt and we started for the stairwell. But my heart sank when I heard Günter's rushed footsteps coming up behind us in the parking-lot. I wanted my father to say that there wouldn't be enough room in the sailboat, which wouldn't have been stretching the truth that much. But I knew he wouldn't. Maybe he thought Uncle Günter was coming around. Maybe he was snapping out of it because they were leaving soon.

My father put down the deposit and left his driver's li-
cence with the man at the desk. We got number 45, a blue
two-man laser. Although I knew there would be no problem with three people, I wanted the man at the desk to say
that one of us would have to sit it out. New regulations on
crowding. Even if it was me. But he only nodded his head
and smiled. He helped my uncle and my father lift the boat
off the racks. They carried it over the gravel driveway and
nosed it into the lake. I followed behind with the lifejackets
and tossed them into the cockpit.

"We'll see what we can do today," my father said once
we got started. We began slowly, cutting through the water, tacking our way out of the shallow bay. There were
other boats in the middle of the lake, small, no other blue
ones except ours, different colours cutting across the water
like coloured shark fins. As we made our way to tap into the
stream of wind that swept across the middle of the lake I
noticed that Günter wasn't comfortable out here. In the
sailboat or on the water, I couldn't tell. But I knew right off
that he didn't know anything about sailing. He hadn't
come swimming with the rest of us, either. But he followed
my father's instructions without questioning, where to sit,
how to move with the boat. He tried to show interest by
asking after the boat's mechanics, pointing to the jib and
boom and knocking his knuckles against the top of the cen-
treboard. I wondered why he was out with us, why he'd
come.

Once we got to the middle of the lake I saw his nervousness. He needed to sit quietly for a moment and get his
bearings. My father was at the tiller, the mainsheet in his
left hand. I was at the bow. I liked sailing. I knew how, but
it was my father's love and I never insisted on taking over
the reins. Anything to do with water was my father's love,
and I wondered at how terrible it was that it should kill his
mother the way it had. He offered me the tiller a couple of
times before we got out to open water, but I was happy to

sit up at the bow and watch him work the boat. He was relaxed and smiling, talking loudly against the wind. He'd told me stories about winning this and that cup when he was a kid, when he sailed competitively for big prizes on lakes with wonderful names like Ammersee and Konigsee, all mysterious mountain lakes in Bavaria, close to Italy. He'd told me stories of all the great yachtsmen he'd met at the Rome Olympics, where he'd finished fifth in the Dragon class.

He pulled us in as close to shore as we could get without crossing the buoys that marked off the swimmers' area to make a pass by Monika, Ruby and my mother. We waved until they saw us and Ruby stood and jumped up and down and cupped her hands around her mouth and yelled something I couldn't make out. Monika hoisted her wine glass above her head and held it there like the Statue of Liberty. We jumped over some small water as we veered out to the middle of the lake. I dragged my hand under the waves, watching my fingers turn pale yellow and then dark like a fish. My hair blew around my face. Günter was smiling now. They were talking back and forth in German, but I could only hear the ghosts of their voices because of the sail flapping against the wind. The gold medal count, my fish, our empty swimming-pool, my uncle, even Monika. It was all gone now. The feeling of jumping over the water, watching people speed by in the other sailboats, red and yellow with small suns stitched into their sails, waving to them as we sped by. The air was hot, even with the wind on us and the misting spray coming up off the bow.

As we approached the end of the lake where I'd caught my fish, I pointed to the cove to show my father and he suddenly, unexpectedly tacked to starboard and I went over the side. I didn't have my life preserver on. I saw the yellow-black rocks come up quick against me, was stunned into sinking because I thought I was still pointing toward the inlet about to say "Trout heaven, full steam ahead" but

I couldn't because my mouth was spreading with lake water and I was sinking. The thought of my grandmother washed over my eyes, how she must have seen the same thing, weeds and rocks, pulled under by the weight of her yellow-and-green wedding-dress, cloaked in water. Then a large, scaly hand descended from above and grabbed me by my right arm and pulled me back into air. I breathed. It pulled me up and laid me across the side of the boat. The sail dropped. We were stopped dead in the water. I started hacking up skunky water from my lungs, spitting up over the edge of the boat. I turned my face up to the sail's small stitched sun and found my uncle looking over me, his entire upper body black from the water, his hair dripping, my father's face white, terrified as it had been the day his mother disappeared into the Trent-Severn Waterway the day of her second wedding. Holding fast the tiller, stopped dead in the water. Saved by my uncle, the plasterer.

I was okay by the time we got home late that afternoon. I'd sunk. I'd swallowed some water, that was it. Günter saved my life and my father came close to seeing his son drown a year after his own mother. But only almost; that was it. Nothing happened, I told myself. I sat in the back seat on the way home, my hand on my father's shoulder the whole way. He'd told my mother, but down-played the accident. She knew I'd fallen in. I told her I'd had my life-jacket on. Günter. I owed him one. China hadn't won a single medal so far. But in their culture, I knew my life was his now.

Over the next two days Ruby and I circled the pool as our uncle worked, so expectant that we forgot about the Games entirely. Günter finished the job two days before my birthday, three days before they were to catch their plane back to Munich. The blue paint he'd finished with needed twenty-four hours to dry. I counted on the clock exactly when I could turn on the hose, desperate for water in my own backyard. I was counting on an Indian summer. It was already September. Ruby and I were going back to school next week. My father had said it didn't make sense filling the pool this time of year. I knew he was right when he told me that, at best, we'd only get a couple of weeks' use out of it. It wouldn't be worth the chemicals we'd have to pour in. But I played up the fact that I was turning fifteen in a few days and that I'd never had a birthday without a swim in the pool. It was a family tradition, I said. But I also knew he wanted to see if all the work Uncle Günter had put in down there had paid off, all the waiting.

I turned on the hose the night before I turned fifteen. The pool was half full by morning. That afternoon we prepared my trout on the barbecue. We'd cleaned them and put them in the freezer because nobody had felt like cooking the night we got home from the lake. We ate hamburgers along with the fish and, for dessert, a chocolate cake that Ruby had helped my mother make. Fifteen blue and red candles sticking out the top. I made a wish and blew once as hard as I could. The flames lowered like sails under a hard wind, tipped and drowned in the white icing. But one remained upright. I licked my finger and thumb, prepared to snuff it out, but Günter quickly leaned over the table and blew it down.

After lunch, around mid-afternoon, we staged our own Olympics. Ruby and I got our bathing-suits on. Our somersaults over the grass that day were as high as they had ever been. Monika called out scores along with my parents while Uncle Günter sat and watched. On my hands I walked from the rock garden to the deck, up onto the diving-board, waited a moment, savouring, and slid smoothly, finally, into the cold water. The pool reached around my body like an animal and squeezed me into a tight ball and for a moment, briefly, my grandmother came back to me. I remembered her down here, the way she must have spent her last conscious seconds before she passed out. I imagined her

97

wedding jewellery sparkling in the dark lake water like underwater treasures. I opened my eyes and saw the faint traces of my uncle's repairs crawling up the sloping sides of the pool like the vines of aquatic flowers.

I dared Ruby to jump in that day. "You'll get used to it," I told her, splashing outwards with an open palm. She stood on the diving-board, a game of ours from the summer before, playing it up for the adults as they sat at the picnic table, drinking their coffee and apple schnapps. She stepped back, took a running jump and arced through the air, hung against the real sun, my little sister, the future gymnast, and broke the water with a delighted screech. Monika smiled and raised her glass over her head. From the water I saw my uncle leave the picnic table.

After dinner we turned on the TV for the first time in two days. So far Canada had only won three bronze and a silver. We were hoping for news of gold. The Games were closing soon. We didn't have much time. At nine o'clock we settled in the TV room to watch the day's highlights, Ruby in the beanbag, my mother with her knitting, my father leafing through *Wind and Sail*. News footage lit up the room. There was a shot of an airport, then masked men and helicopters. Monika was sitting in the rocking-chair beside Ruby. Uncle Günter came in from the front porch, where he'd been sitting with his back against a pillar, reading a copy of *Stern* since dinner. I made a space for him on the couch. I felt the heat come off him when his thigh touched mine.

"You're from there," Ruby said, grabbing Monika's hand when she heard the voice-over say Fürstenfeldbruck. The announcer said the Munich Olympiad had been suspended today at 3:45. The Israeli team was withdrawing. Günter leaned forward, the magazine rolled in his hand. There was a shot of flags flying at half mast. His eyes rolled back into his head like they'd done the day he inhaled the dry dusty earth of my mother's garden. Then the voice-over again said that eleven Israelis had been killed, a Munich sergeant and five terrorists. My mother's hands fell open. Then we saw the pictures of stockinged faces peering around corners, guns in the air. As we watched she translated for her brother, her voice softly floating beneath the glow of the screen. Günter's face didn't change. Ruby didn't understand what they were talking about. "What does hostage mean? What's *hostage!*"

"Prisoner," I said. Then the footage of men in masks, a man throwing a hand grenade into a helicopter as it sat on the tarmac, its still propellers hanging low to the ground like the branches of the elm tree I'd stood under while watching Monika. There was a moment's pause before it exploded. The room filled with the same drowning yellow rays of sun I'd seen at the lake before my uncle's arm pulled me back to the surface, came off the helicopter's black and white explosion.

"Okay, that's enough," my mother said angrily, rolling the ball of wool from her lap. She put down her knitting-needles, took Ruby by the wrist and led her upstairs. "I don't want to be a hostage," I heard her say as she stomped her feet up the stairs beside my mother. "Don't you treat me like a hostage!" My mother came back down a few minutes later. She didn't say anything. She looked at her brother.

"*Juden!*" he said then and smiled. He rolled his fish eyes back around from the inside of his head toward me, as if I was to understand something that no-one else could. He laughed something in German I didn't understand and slapped the rolled up magazine down against my thigh. My mother shot her head around to him again and looked at him icily. Didn't he own me now? I thought. Rocks came up at me, my lungs filled. His hand was warm on my leg. My father put his hands on his knees, about to step between them, his wife and his brother-in-law. Monika was ready to speak. Then I saw something in her eyes that told me this was between brothers and sisters. Not husbands and wives. Not Israelis and Germans and Palestinians. This was about the salt that had pervaded their lives and drained the life from their father, kept the scent of death from the door that June in 1944. This was about cattle cars and blizzards. This was about the heart of my family. Monika was not blood. She would have her turn at him upstairs, alone. Somewhere else. Not here. She would speak to him for the first time in weeks, maybe years. But my mother just got up and left the room. I heard the door to her knitting-room close behind her upstairs. Then Monika left the room and walked out onto the porch. I watched her through the front window. She leaned into a rose that clung to the trellis, a darker hole in the night grid, and her chest filled with fresh air. My father turned off the TV and led me upstairs to bed. From my room I heard him across the hall with my mother, speaking softly. I imagined Ruby lying in bed, drawing the word hostage in the air with a finger. The vacation was over. Tomorrow, they'd be gone.

After everyone had gone to bed, I got up to pee. I stood over the sound of spilling water, still half asleep, and remembered what my uncle was leaving behind for us—a full pool, a wound in the earth shining in the moonlight. I went downstairs, through the kitchen and into the dark sunroom that opened onto the backyard and found Günter in the pool. From the doorway, I watched him swim, his long arms powering him through the water, back and forth like a man pacing the length of a small room. I walked out onto the damp grass and crouched in the shadows by the rock garden. For an hour and more I waited like that, expecting him to go under. I pulled a piece of crab grass from the lawn and sucked the stalk while I watched his darkened figure move through the water. Then I felt the first drop of rain to fall in eight weeks, a light sprinkle, and now the sky swirled and it began to pour. The pool jumped alive and bubbled. I stabbed my tongue into the warm rain, savouring the end of our drought, and formed a cup with my hands. Günter called out to me then. But I didn't answer. What if he'd passed something onto me? I thought. What if, at the lake, my life had passed into his hands when he pulled me from the water? And again, through the rain, he called out to me. I waited, afraid to answer, then raised my cupped hands to my lips and drank.

When She Flew

How far back did it go? This need to leave the world behind, spinning on its blind course.

First, maybe, Ruby's doctor offering her up to air and light. Our mother too exhausted to do more than briefly widen her eyes and smile, then lie back on her pillow at the memory of pain in her body. Held aloft to the light for inspection, she would have opened her arms in the anticipation of flight, hands and fingers arched, cocked for ascent. Days later in the car on the way home from hospital, she would have cupped her hands against forward motion and felt the movement of air blowing in through the open window invisible against her skin. What this was and how it moved objects she must have already known somewhere deep inside her, this great wonder as a forming hand reached for the open window, plied itself upon the wind.

All this, maybe from our grandmother, Lottie, the Olympic diver. The first of the family to take to the clouds. She had tasted the secret of flight, somehow held this in the veins, formulated anew in my new sister on her way home with Mother and Father and me.

Our grandparents saw each other for the first time at the '36 Olympics. That day the Canadian team entered the stadium under the Union Jack, right arms raised in honour of their host. She was eighteen. She'd been the best diver in her native province of Bavaria. On a good day she spun three revolutions and a full body twist before entering water. At twenty-four, my grandfather was one of the best yachtsmen, eight-metre class, in Europe. He was a poor man playing a rich man's game and wore the deceit better than anyone ever knew. His smile was as wide and shining as his yachting ducks, his fingernails carefully manicured and buffed to disguise his cobbler's trade. He was one of the boys. But Lottie knew him for what he was, she said, because Berlin was bedecked with red and black flags by then; it wasn't very hard to see the truth behind all the pomp, in cities or people. They competed on different days. On the morning before he was to sail, my grandfather dressed in his thick cobbler's trousers and boots and walked through the Olympic Village. He found a seat by the pool and waited for my grandmother to walk out onto the ten-metre diving platform above his head. Then she appeared. She balanced on the tips of her toes, spread her arms out in front of her and lifted into air. As she hugged her chest and spun, my grandfather shifted and felt the small finishing nails that he'd forgotten to remove from his pockets prick against his thighs.

My father was a naval engineer and storm hunter. He also knew the power of wind. But there was something practical in how he understood this. I saw it in the way he yearned for tangible results. The uprooting of telephone poles, the movement of 40-foot yachts over weather-chopped water, leaning, bowing to the wind. Nothing thrilled him more than a house expanding and shuddering under the pressure of high winds, or a waterspout dancing over the green waters of Lake Simcoe, my hand in his, sweating, trying to pull away.

Ruby would lie in her crib under a floating mobile of snowflakes cut from paper napkins, their sharp corners sagging with August heat, reaching, reaching. Outside, chickadees gamed among the maples. On a cloudless day of her first summer, she moved her arms, beat against the mattress, kicked her legs, arched her neck until tears fanned across her cheek. Her small body complied, rose in flight and she tasted one of those snowflakes on her tongue, suspended five feet above her crib, spinning lazily. She swore it to me like this. Barely three months in this world, she felt air breathe beneath the small of her back as she rose. *I flew that day*, she said to me, *I know because that snowflake was cold!*

There were many stories like that. In 1970 I was the older brother who listened to Ruby tell her stories of levitation and flight. She was convinced. But she had nothing to back up her claim other than the stories my mother recounted at breakfast over our favourite cereal. *At Loblaws yesterday I left Ruby sitting snug in the shopping-cart, staring up at the cereal on the top shelf. When I got back a second later the cart was full of Fruitloops. Overflowing. No-one else around to help her up there.* And Ruby, smiling then, pushing her bowl to the centre of the table for more. Or the elastic-powered bamboo propeller plane that my grandmother gave me. One morning, after it got stuck in the branches of the highest maple on our street, I ran back to the house to fetch our father. When we returned, the ladder clanking between us, we found Ruby holding the plane in her teeth, still moving her arms like a butterfly.

I had no reason not to believe. I had already performed my own small miracle. In the tub one day, after cleaning my knees of grass stains, my ears of wax, I lay back in the water and placed my eyes on the soapy horizon, observing the small rising coast of my body breathe against the lapping tide. I went under and stayed like that until I felt myself breathe. Underwater, my chest rose and fell, even down there. I believed gills formed on my neck, just below my ears. Looking up through the surface of the water, I wondered at the foreign world of air above, the place my sister inhabited.

We believed we were a gifted family. We were Olympians. No miracle seemed misplaced on us. By that summer, I knew that normal people did not fly, could not breathe under water. But we did. I believed we were evolving. At night I read to Ruby all the dinosaur books I could find at the Centennial Public Library. We pored over artists' interpretations of the first creatures to take to dry land.

Pictures of foraging dinosaurs and the slow erection of man on the evolutionary chart, from monkey-dog to Homo sapien. Beside the last figure, we drew ourselves: a winged angel and a web-footed frogman. Television helped. Captain Kirk, though still able to bleed blood-red, floated like a bird through airless seas. He was the triumph of evolution, a reunion of flyer and amphibian. What he was we were quickly moving toward.

The gifts our family possessed were endless then it seemed. My father's sailing ships never sank—so much as sprang a leak. The clothing my mother sewed for us with fine-boned hands protected us from all weather, even the tornadoes my father and I ventured into. We were always warm and dry, even on the coldest, dampest days. Our grandparents delivered the bushels of ripe fruit they'd plucked from orchards north of Kingston. My father's father cobbled shoes and told Ruby and me you could know a lot about a man from what he wore on his feet. What sort of ground he liked to walk on, where he'd been, where he was likely to go. But we were leaving the earth behind. Already then.

Where they'd been was far away. Germany was an Olympic country. Later we discovered it was a great criminal to be reckoned with, a dumb beast still fumbling in a pool of prehistoric muck. Grateful of the distance between it and ourselves, Ruby and I refused its language. Even when we could not help but understand we turned blank stares to our mother and father when they spoke to us in German. *Was willst Du, Junge? Bist Du müde?* The simplest interrogative, the most necessary offer of food, we met with hungry, staring eyes. We were obstinate. After years, they relented. Even our grandparents saw that their efforts were in vain, realized this new language we used between ourselves was air and light. In the end they spoke to us and the new world around them in strong curving accents. *Vhen ve ver young,* they'd say, *ve alszo flew.*

Our first trip to the museum, we watched the evolution of the world. In glass cases we observed bubbling tar pits swallow our ancestors. Uncle Günter, my mother's brother from Germany, came along that day. Ruby and I ran ahead to the next display, the adults, already tired of this visit, walking behind slowly through dark corridors. They'd reverted to their old language. Between my uncle's weak mumblings, the taped cries of pterosaurs echoed from speakers hidden under plastic ferns and hatching plaster of Paris eggs. This was Ruby's domain. At the flight exhibit, she reached down into the pen for a fallen albatross feather and placed it in her hair. Our uncle thought she was playing Indian. He said in his broken English, "I am Cowboy" and pretended to ride his horse between a group of Japanese. Sneering, Ruby turned back to the albatross and measured its wingspan against her outstretched arms.

I sought traces of marine life: Ichthyosaur and Gryodus, creatures bearing a greater resemblance to my family history than this strange uncle from Germany. Their skeletons swam against a wall of rock, bathed in shimmering light that represented a wind played on prehistoric seas. I did not fight the illusion. I imagined diving down there among my predecessors, long-toothed and free. My hands had once resembled the fins of a dolphin.

Already I saw the great distance forming between my sister and me. We were evolving, but in different directions. Everyone else stood still. That day, she ran back to the flight exhibit after seeing the mummy. I knew the possibility of death had unhinged her. No-one had seen her sneak off. "Back this way," my father said, guessing. We followed him to the second floor and found her sitting on the back of the albatross, suspended ten feet in the air by gleaming wires, the feather in her hair, riding the bird as if it were a winged horse. A Japanese couple took pictures before security came with a ladder and brought her down.

"How did you get up there?" the uniformed man asked,

standing in a nest of osprey eggs. Then to my father, "Who helped her up?" Ruby smiled and pointed to the feather in her hair.

That was an Olympic summer. She was eleven. She'd already seen Olga Korbut reach for the ceiling in Munich. She thought it was all perfectly normal. But as Ruby's talents soared, the gifts my family possessed began to fade. The summer before, my grandmother had died in a boating accident. She drowned in front of the whole family on the day of her thirty-fifth wedding anniversary wearing the green and yellow dress that my mother had made especially for that day. Now my grandfather was alone in Kingston. The following spring, my father was informed that one of the sailboats he'd designed went down off the southern tip of St. Lucia. I was growing faster than our mother could sew. There was no choice but to wear clothing bought from a store. I was cold and damp the whole winter of '72.

Ruby started training three days a week at the gym with a part-time gymnastics coach named Sarah. Before long, she was competing. That was when my mother started talking about losing a daughter for all the time she spent swinging from the uneven bars, away at meets around the province, sometimes in Quebec and New York and Michigan. In the spring, Ruby cleaned up at the provincials and got the attention of Dan Weise, the coach of the national team. He said she had a rare talent. There was still time to make her into a world-class gymnast. I went to the gym with her after school and watched her train. Dan stood to one side of the mat she was working over, wringing his hands together and yelling, *push, more air, harder, yes* then *flying!* clapping once and arching his back as she let go of the bar, spinning upwards. "We're going to have to take the ceiling off if you go any higher," he said that day.

Then later. "There's talent here," he said sitting at the kitchen table, cutting into the cake that my mother had placed in front of him. "Tremendous talent." My father told him about the Olympic blood in our veins. He showed him pictures of my grandmother and grandfather standing together in Berlin, one of those red-and-black flags and a man in jack-boots caught in the background. And his own pictures of Rome.

"Josef," Dan said. He put down his fork and took the Berlin photograph in his hand. "What are we going to do? You know something like this requires commitment."

"Elizabeth?" said my father. My mother was at the sink, rinsing out the coffee filter. Her wedding ring sat on the counter-top, a safe distance away from the sink. She turned around, hands still dripping.

"I'm not prepared to lose my daughter to someone else's lost dream."

Dan and my father looked at each other across the table. I knew my father. *Give it time*, his face said, then winked a knowing eye. Dan understood. He gave the picture back to my father and silently returned to his cake.

A week later, my mother took Ruby aside. She held her small callused palms in her hands and looked at them sadly. "Is this what you want? Leather hands. The hands of a 60-year-old woman before you're twelve."

"I want to fly," she answered, and my mother got up from the edge of my sister's bed and left the room in tears. That's what did it for my mother, I think, this turning away from her to something she did not understand. She was not an Olympian. Evolution was not hers. Most of her family had died, been killed in war or left to languish among the ruins only to visit here with memories of what she had left behind. But Ruby's was a flight forward, all of us but our mother could see that.

My father and I chased storms now more than ever. We understood wind speed and air pressure in a different way than my sister did. We monitored the Ontario Weather Centre, always on the lookout for severe weather. Tornadoes were our jackpot. Together, we dreamed about tornado hunting becoming an Olympic sport. Sometimes we'd be gone entire weekends looking for storms. My father took off work when something was brewing on the horizon. Sometimes we'd drop Ruby off at the gym in Burlington on our way out to the storms. From the car the three of us would wave to my mother on the doorstep as we pulled out of the driveway, the look of sadness and confusion already marked across her forehead, and she would wave back and stand with her arm in the air until we turned onto Lakeshore and headed west.

Next, the games themselves. When she flew. Ruby's Team Canada uniform arrived in the spring. Despite our protests, she refused to try it on for fear that it carried a spell that wore off with each donning. It was red with white stripes down the side, a small maple leaf on the right shoulder. A woman from the local paper came to our house two weeks before she left for Montreal. She asked my sister what the games meant to her. She said her ambition was to fly like she'd seen Olga Korbut do four years earlier.

The first day of the women's gymnastics competition we watched her walk across the mats and mingle with the other gymnasts. She bounced up and down on the floor-mat a few times, then at the vault, testing the air. The Forum was at capacity. We were in the reds, beside a couple from New York. I told them my sister was down there. "The blond ponytail," I said, pointing. "In the red suit." As she warmed up, the hair fastened at the back of her head bounced like a bird's wing.

"She must be good," the woman said.

"She can really fly."

"I heard the one to watch is a little Romanian."

My mother was wringing her hands. She'd left the knitting-bag she usually carried at the hotel. My father was talking a mile a minute to anyone in earshot, sometimes looking down at his fingers as he fed film into his camera. He leaned across my mother's lap.

"Doesn't she look grand down there," he said to the couple beside me. "Look at her!" and they both nodded generously. "The little Olympian."

Before her first event, Ruby fidgeted on the bench. I knew she was re-running her routines over and over in her head, perfecting each twist and arch in her mind one last time. I prayed she'd repeat those routines she'd mapped out in her head so perfectly. I watched her small heaving chest fill with anticipation when her number was called. There was flight in her step, more elegant than any of us had ever seen before. Dan smiled, nervously running the zipper of his tracksuit up and down over his chest. He arched his neck as she walked across the floor. Other events continued around her. She stood, paused at the top of the runway, stepped one foot back, bent a knee, waited and exploded down the mat. She hit the springboard with a boom and rose to meet the vault, twisting, touching the horse leather, popping once again into air as my father's camera clicked, then nailed a double full body twist. She straightened her back and threw her head toward us, smiling.

There were no new medals on the fireplace mantel after Montreal. Ruby was barely twelve. She'd been training for just four years; she'd competed against the best in the world. When she got back, there were receptions and what they called "wind-down" meets. She talked a lot about Moscow. On weekends my grandfather still visited, but not as often as he had when our grandmother was alive and, when he did come, he no longer brought with him bushels of apples and peaches and pairs of leather shoes. That year brought a warm fall, but Ruby hurried my mother in the preparation of more hand-knit sweaters. "Make it thicker," she'd say of a sweater-in-progress, testing the Angora wool against her cheek. She wore my mother's sweaters when the rest of us were still wearing T-shirts. Into the third week of an Indian summer, a boy from up the street told me that girls wore baggy clothes to hide their flat chests. That fall Ruby did her homework in front of the fireplace. She went to bed early almost every night.

"It's fatigue. She's coming down from Montreal," my father said. I'd heard him talking to Dan on the phone. "I remember feeling like that after Rome." But she was losing strength. She'd started sitting out practice. Her teachers called, hinting at family problems.

On a Tuesday in December, back for lunch, I found my mother slouched over at the kitchen table. She got up and held me in her arms. Tears ran on her cheeks. "We were at the doctor's this morning," she said. "Ruby's sick."

I waited a moment. "With what?"

"She's got something in her blood," she said angrily in a voice that surprised and frightened me. Her left hand started to shake. I took hold of her arm and sat with her. I poured tea into the cup she'd been hanging her head over when I first saw her. Then she told me of the blood test Ruby'd just had.

I watched my mother's face as she spoke. She was looking around herself for strength. I knew I wasn't what she needed right then. I went to the living-room and called my father at work but they told me he was already on his way. I replaced the receiver and went upstairs. Ruby was in her room, sitting upright against the headboard of her bed, the pink duvet my mother had made for her the year before pulled up over her legs.

"Booby?" I took her hand and rubbed the leather pads on her palms. She was looking out the window at the sparrows in the maple trees. "Tell me the story again about the first time you flew."

Nothing was confirmed until the spinal tap that night. In her hospital-room, I held Ruby's hand when the doctor stuck her with the butterfly needle. She already had an IV hooked up to her right arm. She cried out and pulled my arm into her chest. My mother touched her forehead. "It hurts now," my father said, wincing. "But they've got to find out what's wrong." There were coloured posters of Big Bird and Aquaman on the wall across from the bed. I saw the white liquid slowly fill the cylinder the nurse had attached to the needle.

My mother stayed with her in the hospital that night. My father and I drove home in silence. It was before eight when we pulled into the driveway. I went straight to the Centennial Public Library and got out all the books I could find on dinosaurs and the evolution of birds.

The chemo started the next day. Every morning she was given drugs with prehistoric names like Vincristine and Prednisone. They were trying to get her into remission. "Ruby," I said that first afternoon, *The Riddle of the Dinosaur* cradled in my arm. "You wanna hear about *Archaeopteryx?*" Without waiting for her answer, I sat down beside her on the bed.

"...*stonecutters in Bavaria*—which is where we were last summer—*made one of the most fascinating discoveries of all time*." I paused and looked up at Big Bird. Ruby was staring out the window into the trees.

"They found the fossil remains of what looked like a reptile, possibly a small dinosaur, that in some respects bore a resemblance to a bird, for it had feathers. Darwin had hypothesized that birds must have developed from reptiles, and there was the evidence, so it seemed, in the reptile-bird known as Archaeopteryx. Evolutionists could scarcely believe their good fortune."

After school I visited her in her room and read to her about the emergence of flying creatures. She was losing weight fast. Soon most of the veins in her arms had collapsed from the IV. By the end of the first week, the nurses were forced to move to the veins in her feet to hook her up. She had nothing left in her arms. After I read to her about the existence of the Archaeopteryx, the bird-reptile, I read to her the accounts of the discoveries of the London, Berlin, Maxburg, Teyler and Eichstatt specimens. At night I remembered the evolutionary charts we had drawn in, the winged angel she always drew beside my frog-man.

I tried to get her to talk. To bring her out of her pain. To give her somewhere to go.

"It's about us coming back together again," I said. "The same evolutionary path."

After thirteen days of intensive chemo, Ruby came home. She'd lost close to fifteen pounds. There were poke marks in her back from the repeated spinal taps. Her skin looked like the mottled hide of an *Ankylosaur*. Within a month, she ballooned. The vincristine kept her eating all day long. I wondered if I was the only one to see how they were hurting her. I found clumps of hair on her pillow. By evening, transparent blond balls of hair tumbled across the living-room floor at the slightest push of air. She had sores on her face. The smallest infection could send her back to hospital. Whenever she went outside, she wore a surgical mask. The doctors said she had to wait until her poly count reached 1,000 before she could move freely in crowds.

Three times a week, we drove to Toronto Sick Kids for chemo and blood tests. We began to think numbers. We sat in the waiting-room for the hour it took Ruby to go through the procedure. The doctors said she was in the group they called "average risk," which was someone her age with a white blood cell count of less than 50,000. My father, the optimist, said the best minds in the world were on top of this one. "She's being cured right now, as we speak," he'd say. Near the end of the session he'd leave and come back with a dozen Tim Hortons donuts for us to eat on the way home.

That winter, the house grew brittle with sickness. We

were all cold. Ruby seemed to bruise at the mention of touch. The muscle that had once helped her fly was now gone. I saw in her eyes and the way she walked what the last few months had done to her, her back hooked like an old woman's to suit her leathery hands. There was no bounce in her step. Her small body, once clean and powerful, was now frightening to look at. Wherever she went she left clumps of hair like balls of tangled transparent fishing-line.

Storms came and went without my father's notice. In May someone from the Weather Centre called to ask why we'd missed the tornado that had ripped up the bridge over the Ganaraska. When my father told them what was happening, no-one called again. *There's storm enough here*, I knew he was thinking. Quilts floated like magic blankets from my mother's sewing-room. The fire blazed that winter; but somehow, it couldn't warm the chill in our veins.

In March, after four months of chemo, the maintenance therapy started. Just after Ruby's thirteenth birthday. I would turn seventeen that summer. Things began to level out. Most of the time Ruby was fine, except for the few days a month when she had to take her drugs. I read books on leukemia. It was called the children's cancer. I'd hoped an understanding of the disease would give us the upper hand. I left the books on my parents' bed before saying goodnight. I remembered my father's refrain from our storm-hunting days. *In scientia est salus.* In knowledge is safety. It had proven wrong already. But it was the only thing I could do. Study and learn. My mother made blankets to keep Ruby from more harm. They covered her like a protecting skin. My father sat by her bed from the moment he returned from the shop until she fell asleep. My grandfather came on the train from Kingston as often as his failing health permitted. Among the books I signed out from the library were more studies of evolution.

I had already applied to the University of Chicago, where I hoped eventually to study advanced meteorological sciences under the eminent weather theorist, Professor Fujita. But by then I'd dropped severe weather as a hobby and turned to paleontology. I'd dissected Darwin's *The Origin of Species* and considered every theory and counter theory that it had spawned over the last 119 years, hoping that a pattern in our small lives would emerge against the backdrop of time.

And, for a time, it worked. Within a year, Ruby responded to her treatment. She was strong again. Her hair came back, a blond curly mass. By mid-winter, she was on the road to complete remission. The count of leukemic blasts seemed to be bottoming out. Every week she went in for blood tests. The chemo was tapered off to nothing. I felt magnanimous. I wanted to celebrate. Into her second spring as an outpatient, I resolved to raise money for The March of Dimes. The same day I started working on a plan to break the world drown-proofing record, I went canvassing for sponsorships. Ruby helped me train. I'd already been in contact with Guinness. In May she walked back and forth on the deck of the pool timing my laps, egging me on, slapping her thigh, shouting when I began to tire. She was back on a modest training program, herself. She was talking about Moscow again. There was no reason why she couldn't go. She had a year and a half before the Nationals.

That summer her spirit soared in anticipation of her body. She took to the air again after almost two years of treatment and recovery. My parents and I sat at the picnic table before supper and watched her perform a tentative flip or a handstand, then lower herself into the splits, beaming up at us as if she was performing these moves for the very first time.

"Careful," my mother would say, more out of habit than fear.

"Look, Boobs," I said, when she finally sat down at the picnic table. "Do either of us have any excuse now?"

"*Nyet,*" she said, leaning into my father's chest. We were back on track after some minor evolutionary setbacks. Our mother began making clothes again after a year and a half of blankets. There hadn't been any problems with my father's sailboats since the disappearance off St. Lucia more than two years ago. Our summer hummed with the sound of a Laser cutting through perfect wind and water, the jib finely tuned to the world.

Ruby returned to school that fall after we floated down the Joshua on a clock without hands, and in October she started in earnest at the gym. Dan talked to my parents about it, and to the doctors at Sick Kids. He wanted to know how hard he could push her. My mother bit her lip and frowned; the doctors assured her that it was best for a recovering patient to get back into the routine of his or her normal life once a complete remission was at hand. Physical exercise would just help the process along. Her red blood cell count was normal; there was little or no fear of anaemic reactions.

There were small gym meets that winter. Ruby watched from the bleachers. She still wasn't a hundred percent. Her friends spun through the air over her head, twisting. She wasn't jealous. It made her work harder. Before she could take to the uneven bars, she remapped her routines over and over in her mind, flew higher than she'd even flown before. "I'm refuelling," she'd say. Clouds raced through her head.

In the summer of that year, she competed for the first time in two and a half years. The doctors at Sick Kids predicted a complete remission. In the Ontario championships, Ruby took gold in floor and vault and pulled in the bronze for total points. We were all there to watch. Even my mother started thinking Moscow.

Three weeks after the meet, Ruby developed a sore throat. For two days we watched the cough. Then they took her to Toronto for her weekly tests. I saw them off that morning. Two hours later I heard the car pull into the driveway. I was doing lengths in the pool. Ruby came around back and kicked off her sneakers and sat on the grass and started singing a Bee Gees song she'd just heard on the radio. Then she went upstairs to get into her bathing-suit.

My mother and father came out into the backyard and sat down on the deck. My father leaned over and touched the water with his finger. "Warm," he said, considering something. "Peter. She's out of remission."

"But they said they got all the blasts."

"There's been a relapse. They said it takes only a few leukemic cells to take over the whole body again. Her red-cell count's taken a nose-dive. She's having an anaemic re-action. That explains the cough. Dr. Lee says there's an operation she has to have if they can get her into remission again. It's a transplant. It's the last option. He needs to take something out of your hip and give it to Ruby."

I rested my chin in my hands on the wooden deck, the noon sun warming my shoulders. I'd read a dozen books on leukemia by now. I kicked my feet behind me and raised my body parallel to the surface. I knew what was coming.

"That's where the blood's made," my mother said. "It's called bone marrow." She touched my arm. "They kill all of the bone marrow cells in Ruby, and give her some of your healthy cells. Not just the leukemic ones. They destroy everything. It's best if it's a brother or a sister. That's the best chance she's got. Then she starts producing her own. But they have to test your blood to see if you're compatible. If you are, you could do it."

The screen door slid open then and Ruby walked onto the patio in her bathing-suit. She didn't look sick to me. She looked tan and healthy. She still didn't know about the relapse. I climbed out of the pool.

"Ruby, it's back," my mother said. She understood, just from that, and sat down at the edge of the pool, her feet hanging motionless in the water, and cried.

By suppertime she was back at the hospital and on chemo again, hooked up to the IV, her head sideways on the pillow, turned toward the sky on the other side of the window. There was another spinal tap that night. When they pulled out the big butterfly needle, a nurse called me into the next room for my blood sample.

Within a week they determined we had nearly identical HLA antigens. There was a match.

Then, the radiotherapy. We watched her on the video monitor, her head strapped down to the flat surface to prevent any movement. Beside us in the booth, the technician gave Ruby some last-minute instructions over the microphone. "Remember, honey. Absolutely still, okay?" The hum of heavy, slow-moving machines. On the lead-covered door a sign read CAUTION—HIGH RADIATION AREA. The woman looked at me and mouthed, *All right.*

I brought my face close to the microphone and began to read.

"*One day in 1802, a college student named Pliny Moody, while plowing his father's field in South Hadley, Massachusetts, turned up a sandstone slab bearing the imprint of a large three-toed foot. It looked like the footprint of a giant turkey or raven.*" I looked up at the screen and said, "You copy? Over." I waited.

Over the speaker we heard her thin, metallic voice. "I copy."

"*Those who saw this wonder decided, in a moment of pious fancy, that the print must have been made by the raven that Noah had released from the arc to search for dry land.*"

"Only a few minutes, honey," my father said, his face pressed against mine. They'd said there was no pain involved. She was laced to the earth like a helpless Gulliver. When the hum of the machines died, the technician went into the chamber and turned Ruby over. She came back out and started the radiation again.

"Other tracks of Noah's raven were found over the years, always in the Triassic sandstone that would become the source of the 'brownstone' favoured in the construction of Manhattan townhouses."

"Would you like to see that some day, Ruby?" my mother asked into the microphone. "Go to America to see dinosaur fossils in the houses there?"

"I want it to stop," she said, weakly. "Over."

Three weeks of this, roped to the hard board in the radiation-room. She lost weight rapidly. Her hair fell out again. She was back to where she started. Everyday, radiotherapy. I wondered if she carried around the poison rays once they'd turned off the machine. A fire cooking inside her body.

"All this is going somewhere," I told her. "Archaeopteryx didn't know he was turning into a bird when it was happening." There were dark circles under her eyes. Her head looked too big for her body. I didn't know if she understood what I wanted her to understand.

"What a funny thing I'll turn out to be," she said. "This mix, you and me."

A week before the transplant was set to go, I wrote the Dean of Sciences at the University of Chicago to ask for a deferral. I explained what was happening to my family. In the letter she returned to me, the Dean said she would be pleased to have a student in her faculty as dedicated to family as I seemed to be. She enclosed a *Scientific American* article that touted miraculous advances in leukemia research and treatment. She ended the letter, Godspeed.

Before the operation, I dreamt Ruby and I flew. She carried me on her back. Bathed in sunlight, Lake Ontario opened before us. We broke the surface and went under. As we went deeper and deeper I blew oxygen into my sister's mouth. We found a treasure chest at the edge of an under-water mountain full of syringes and leukemic blasts. We loaded the needles and squeezed their milky substance into the pale water and watched the thinned cancerous blood dissipate through streaked sunlight descended from the surface.

The nurses encouraged me to walk a few hours after I came out of the anaesthetic. Still in my pyjamas, I rode the elevator and limped down the hall to Ruby's room. By the time I got there, she'd already received the first bag of marrow they'd taken from me. It hung on a rack beside the bed, like an IV, but the tube was hooked up directly below her collar bone. The doctor said everything looked good so far. She felt feverish; her head pounded. I felt nauseated. All the side-effects we'd been warned about were there. But the pain in my bones began to subside. It felt like I was carrying gravel in my hips. They did tests before they hooked up a second, paler bag. We waited there with her for the two hours it took to complete the transplant, watching the bags' yellow-pink contents move along the tube and disappear into Ruby's chest, the afternoon sun streaming through the open window. She was kept in isolation to minimize the risk of infection.

After a month, the rejection began. Her body turned red with blotches. Her skin turned scaly. Everyday, after work and school, my father and I drove to Toronto. My mother would be there, waiting. Ruby would ask me to scratch her back when our parents went out to the hallway to consult with Doctor Lee. I'd slide my hand under her shoulder-blades and lightly run my fingers up and down her spine. I felt the drying skin come off in my hand. "Softer," she'd say, and me barely touching her. The tests confirmed it. They called it Graft Versus Host Disease. Her skin burned; the diarrhea threatened to drain all the liquids from her body. I was the graft. It was me doing this to her.

Skeletal now, her shoulder-blades emerging from her body like great wings. Small like a bird and, birdlike, her mind jumping suddenly from post to wire. Her breaths were short. *Yes, scratch there,* she'd say. And then appearing on a branch. *Cold like an icicle! Remember how I told you it was?* And of a sudden, screeching, *I want to go home. Over!* And then fluttering. The final attempts to rise. *Booby,* I'd say, taking the hand.

Helpless that last week, we watched as her thoughts soared. Perched on black-iron weathervanes, surveying, then breaking free in a desperate flutter of wing and feather. When open, her eyes glowed with an understanding gathered from dizzying heights. *How sad, the end of the Triassic,* she said, clawing against air; her voice thin now as her wrists. *Countdown to Moscow.* For days, her body receding along a parade of nurses and doctors. Always my mother or father staying behind while I went home with the other in silence to rest.

"Sweetheart?" my father said that last morning, sinking to his knees. Her clawed hands scratching against air as they might have done her first day in hospital years before. Her small body writhed in its attempt to fly. A desperate fluttering, the straining effort to leave the world beneath her, one last time. Then the quiet stillness, Ruby somewhere distant as my mother, all month fighting tears, hoped for her child's quick death. All of us. We knew what each was thinking. Eagerly now, we waited for silence to come and wrap his dark glove over her heart. My mother, without words, joined my father on her knees as my sister rose, her life finally drifting like windfall over broad water, a red speck of autumn leaf ascending and forever gone.

NADINE MCINNIS

The Lotus-Eater

I try to avoid looking at my reflection in the bus window, a woman holding flowers being ferried across a river at this bleak time of year. Roses in November would be appropriate, I guess. All day I've been going over poetry in my head, figuring out what I will read him tonight in the hospital, discarding the *carpe diem* poems and that old ballad *Barbry Allen* that has been ringing through my head. But I'm not carrying roses. What do you give a man who's dying too fast, too young? I chose fern and one lifting bird of paradise. Not a thousand female folds like carnations or roses. I'll have to keep the flower under wraps when I get home. My husband isn't going with me tonight, and he might ridicule my choice, think it's too theatrical.

I hold his wife's hand in the hospital corridor. The dingy light of November never leaves these halls. This was once a hospital for births and recoveries, but now it is just for the dying. Stepping through the doorway beneath those tons of grey stone walls, I felt that I was entering more than a hospice. I was stepping through a small hole at the base of a tombstone, like a mouse, some scrap of life scurrying furtive and temporary, disrupting nothing much in the larger frame of things.

She's a ghastly grey, maybe twenty pounds lighter than she was in her aqua bathing-suit at last summer's parties. One stone lighter. That sounds right, given what she's going through. There's a whiff of cheap perfume that couldn't possibly be emanating from her at a time like this. Vaguely religious, and then I can identify it. I used to think this was the smell of a blessing, the difference between holy water and ordinary water, before I learned that they perfume the fonts in churches. Here, church and hospital are blurred. The ceilings are so high you almost expect to look up and see clouds. There are narrow recessed windows of leaded glass along the corridor, peaked into sharp points, like steeples. She tells me as if we've been intimate all our lives: "Just a few days more. I can't believe it. How can he go so fast," and she bends her face down to her collar.

"June," I say, suddenly shaken. "Can I do anything for you?" I would like to embrace her but my hands are full; the flower, which I'm ashamed of because it suddenly seems so assertive, so playful, the books in my arms. All the things I'm bringing for him.

"Please feel you can send the kids over anytime. Anytime at all."

"Thank you for coming to sit with him," is all she replies. "I don't want him to be alone, but the children are having a rough time. I have to leave now." She walks away, angled a little sideways, like the slow lope of a wolf. She bumps into the corner before slipping out of sight.

I set the bird of paradise on the table beside his bed. A watery pattern wavers high up on the wall. The shadow of the webbed band of the curtain. The light is so subdued, he could be lying underwater, so quiet, we could both be underwater. He vaguely opens his eyes without registering me. I glance down at my white sweater and realize that I must look like a nurse from his vantage point.

"Robert, I brought you flowers, or a flower, I guess. Actually only one," I stammer, and he focuses his eyes and raises them to my face.

"Oh," he says, almost a moan, then silence, and I realize he's trying to place my face.

"Evelyn. It's your neighbour, Evelyn."

"E-velyn," he says finally, without further comment.

He closes his eyes again, which is a relief, because they look nothing like his blue eyes. Without lashes, they are milky and bare, like pools just beginning to freeze over.

"Can I get you anything. Is there anything you want?" I ask, unable to think of any other possibility. After a moment he raises his arm slightly off the bed, and grins slightly, or maybe it's the pain.

"Everything I need is here." he whispers, directing my gaze to the IV running into his forearm. The nervousness, I don't know, but I laugh. He sinks lower into himself, pleased I think.

"I'll read to you," I say, and he nods.

I feel my voice thin and uncertain as I begin reading *The Lady of Shallot*. I half expect him to tease me, as he always did at parties when I got too serious. "Evelyn, sweetie, lighten up," he'd say, draping a strong arm around my shoulders. A kind of energy swirled around him, a signal his body sent picked up by women. And I would suddenly feel the top of my head lift off, stumble a little out of his reach, blaming the drinks.

We used to walk home together from meetings at the community centre. And he'd tell me things about the inside of every house on the street. Being a carpenter, he knew all the intimate details, having been consulted at every neighbourhood party. Who has a blood-red jacuzzi, who put a skylight in their bedroom. He would nudge close to me, describing windows and frames and plumbing. And sometimes darker secrets too, just hinting at money problems, sexual problems, fist holes through drywall.

Concrete and window-frames were his elements, but people were his talent. He showed me how to wrap the tiny tendrils of the clematis around the trellis. It blew down in a windstorm, and almost broke my heart when I saw it, lying like a long purple spill on the front lawn. He draped the weight of it over my shoulders, purple blossoms tickling the back of my neck, drooping over the top of my head as he wrapped tendrils and tied with string bunches of stems to the wooden trellis. He laughed and told me I looked like I was wearing an ermine-trimmed cape, starting to tie near my ankles, then level with my hips, moving up methodically, relieving me gradually of the weight of the vine on my back, working, knotting near my heart, my neck, and finally tying clematis just behind my head, weaving some of my hair in with the leaves by accident, so that I was caught until he untangled me. "Queen Evelyn," he called me. The delicacy of his fingers, his voice so soothing, coaxing, I couldn't help but let my own small wishes form.

Willows whiten, aspens quiver,
Little breezes dusk and shiver

Instead of laughing, he expels his breath, and waits. Gently, in words spun over one hundred years ago, the world slowly floats by an island where that lonely woman lives. I quickly rush by the funeral procession on its way to Camelot, but he opens his eyes at the lines "'I am half sick of shadows,' said The Lady of Shalott," and he asks me to say it again.

"I am half sick of shadows," said
The Lady of Shalott.

He says, "Yeah," as if he's been waiting a long time to move on, even though it's been only a matter of months since he fell ill.

How can I help but cry then. He's made it real for himself and therefore for me. And I'm crying through her weaving and her mirror, her loneliness, and especially through the blooming water-lily that brings the curse of love to her after she sees Sir Lancelot.

"Thank you," he says when I'm finished, not formal, just weary. "That was nice." Sometime during the poem, he pressed the button on the morphine pump and now begins to slip away from me, lying in a boat gliding down a river with the Lady, my voice trailing at a distance, carried easily across water.

The room wavers before my eyes, I drift up onto weak legs, my coat over my arm keeping me from floating high above his bed, and I hear my voice telling him that I love him. So simple, my voice more steady than I ever would have imagined. Impossible that I've said this out loud. This secret. Every night when his headlights moved across my window, I was happy. Standing there waiting, with green beans in the colander, or the earthy smell of potatoes as I washed them at the sink, looking out through the darkness and my own startled rabbit reflection in the glass.

He doesn't stir.

My heart is still pounding at the bus stop, still pounding as I lie next to my husband all night. I feel so agitated, I must get up and open the door to the hall. Doors have opened everywhere. A door in my life, opening me to him; a door creaking open in his life, moving toward it, away from me. Tossing from side to side, I remember the tunnel of the apartment we lived in when I was pregnant for the first time. Sitting in the dark in the middle of the night, grieving my loss. But how could I miss books with so much life ahead of me? These books I've carried with me from place to place, one on my knee in the hospital. Back then, I sat in the dark living-room, bereft, seeing light seep around the edges of the doors at either end of the long hall. Sheltered in my narrow tunnel of darkness while the public light of the stairwells burned at either end. We were to live our lives in such a narrow, private band of our own making.

I have to go back to the hospital. A repeat of last night. June acknowledges me vaguely in the corridor outside his room. She doesn't seem to resent my intrusion, although she never took much notice of me as a neighbour even before this happened. She always said hello when we met by accident on home territory, but I always had the feeling she wouldn't recognize me outside the neighbourhood. Tonight, she looks slightly more rested. She tells me he was stronger today, that he even ate some broth, first time in five days. That the end sometimes comes after a brief reprieve. She doesn't say *hope*, but I can see that even though the vigil might be longer, she sees this as a kind of gift.

"He won't see anyone now," she tells me. "He told me to keep his parents away. And the children. They can't understand why he's turning them away."

"I didn't realize. I'll just go now."

"You can read to him. Someone should be here, and it can't always be me," she says and turns away as if she is suddenly angry.

"Evelyn," he says softly when he sees me push tentatively through the curtain around his bed.

I'm embarrassed. I avert my eyes, glance down at my hands.

"Look at the flower you brought me. Full glory," he says. I can't bear to look at the bird of paradise; it is too flagrant. When I finally raise my eyes, I see that it is all right. I see the cords, the strange lumps of his neck.

"Are you going to read to me tonight?" he asks.

"If you want. What do you want to hear?"

"Everything just like last night," he tells me, directly. A little of his old self in that. A little of the tease, daring me to take it further, and the sadness just beneath the challenging tone.

"Is this...appropriate?" I ask, feeling the hair prickle on the back of my neck.

"A little late to worry about that," he says. His breath shortens, he seems to have more to say, but instead after a long silence pushes the button on the morphine pump and almost immediately sinks lower in the bed.

"You want me to say it again?" I laugh, I can't help it, and the tears blur along the rims of my eyes.

"I want you to," he says.

"Remember that time we ran into each other on Front Street? Near Christmas. I always feel so lost in crowds, like a refugee."

"Yeah, that's it, like a refugee," he says dopily, opening, then closing his eyes.

I tell him it was mild and his coat was undone at the top. And I wanted to put my lips there. What a shock, I felt it through my whole body. Wanting to put my lips on his throat.

"You felt that way?" he asks.

"Yes," I say, simply I hope, with my hands folded in my lap. I look at him again, not seeing the hairless sunken throat, the yellow skin. He releases himself back into his own weariness, closes his eyes and says, "I want you to tell me."

"Tell you what?"

"Tell me everything."

"Oh. I can't."

"...what you imagined," he says, slurring his speech a little. Perhaps he pushed the button on the pump again. He seems to be drifting off.

I tell him I always imagined no connections. No husbands or wives, no subterfuge. I tell him I pictured us past Cedar Point, him weighing me down in the grass on the riverbank. The weight of him.

He's lying back. Perhaps he is already unconscious. I try to find the words he's asking for.

"What do you want?" I ask him, feeling a little desperate. But his eyes have grown less intense, like some of the light has gone out of them. The drugs taking over.

"Poetry. Just poetry," he says almost under his breath.

I look down at the book in my lap. How could I have been so stupid.

"Tennyson again, then." Suddenly all the poems seem to be about death, not love after all.

"'The Lotos-Eaters,'" I say. He's moved beyond me again. Maybe something of this will reach him, but at one glance I realize it is about death too.

"Courage!" he said, and pointed toward the land,
"This mounting wave will roll us shoreward soon."

And I journey too into the shadowed glades drugged with flowers, wandering along streams, a place I've never been before.

Most weary seemed the sea, weary the oar,
Weary the wandering fields of barren foam.
Then someone said, "We will return no more;"

A sound stops me. Perhaps coming from somewhere in the room, perhaps only from inside my own head. A slippery rasping sound, and I look up. Robert's eyes are open and unfocussed. Then a smooth breath.

"There. Under the trees. An echo," he says.

I lean closer, leaning on the metal rail between us.

"What? What was that, Robert?"

"A mistake," he says.

"No. Not a mistake," I say, the panic rising in my throat.

"Glitters," he says. "You. The echo."

I hear a beating in my left ear. My breath is caught in an endless loop under my sternum, circling like my dizziness.

"I see the river. You're under the trees with me. I'll come with you," I say. A pause. He drowses. "Your hands. Your mouth...."

"So, you've managed to put him to sleep," June says. I must have been whispering softly to him because his wife only touches my shoulder, startling me. Half of me is still lost with him in this forest, expecting no-one to come along.

"I'll leave," I say immediately, standing and knocking the open book of poems off my lap with a bang that seems to echo down all the long corridors.

"That's good of you to read to him. I don't want him to be alone," she says as she sinks into the chair I have vacated. "I don't want to be alone either," she adds, her voice catching.

"It's late," I say, putting on my coat, confused by how difficult it is until I realize I'm starting with the wrong arm. "Do you usually come back this late?"

She looks up at me, and her forehead crumples again, tears fill her eyes.

"It could be tonight," she says, looking at Robert. "I'm sitting through the night. They told me it could be tonight."

"But he was better today," I protest.

"The system's closing down. The body stops fighting itself. That's what they say," and she reaches out and takes his hand. He is inert. Beyond both of us.

How to sleep, startled in unguarded moments by something that feels like joy. Keeping the door open, thinking I see a man standing there blocking the light from the hall when I turn over exhausted. I do not sleep well, but dream anyway. That forest, far off through the trees, and a procession of mourners, all clothed in black from head to toe. The same hot day. I look down and find that I am naked. I can't go near, even though he's there, because I'm not dressed for a funeral.

The phone doesn't ring. Surely she would call. I was the last one to see him conscious. I check with the hospital at noon. Still alive. His death is now only half of what I fear. I fear the phone not ringing. I fear the phone ringing, and hearing her voice, icy and thin, saying:

"How long has it been going on? Two years? Three? No point keeping secrets now."

Her voice, and the dead space on the line after she hangs up.

I wait until the kids are settled in their rooms doing their homework, call out quickly that I have to go out for a little while, and then stand in the gathering dusk, waiting for the next bus. I stumble up the high bus stairs, feeling like a child, though no-one pulls me along and up by the hand. Perhaps I look almost normal if I keep my eyes down, focused on the grey slush pressed into the black rubber ridges. We pass out of the suburbs, onto the lighted, snowy streets, arc over the bridge, the river beneath still unfrozen, but black and thick, slowing down. Once again, through the strange lighted door at the base of this stone monstrosity, nothing in my hands. No flowers, no books. A nurse stops me in the corridor, after a few minutes, knocks discreetly on his closed hospital door.

When June faces me finally, she seems calm.

"Evelyn," she says, holding both my hands, "You've been a good friend." Then she puts her arms around my neck, burying her face in my shoulder. "He slipped into a coma early this morning. It won't be long now. Everyone else has gone home. I'm going to stay."

My face presses against her hair. I'm crying along with her, holding her softness against me, the body he has loved in my arms.

Claiming the Body

My mother has refused to claim and bury the body of her brother. All week, the image of his body wrapped in sheets has threatened to unravel in my mind.

I was informed of my uncle's death as an afterthought to an aimless conversation with my father. I am sure he is drinking although he claims to be sober now. He often calls me in the morning and offers to bring me groceries. This was the third morning in a row he tried to talk me into a crate of cantaloupes.

"You can store them here in the basement fridge," he insisted. "I can bring one over any time." When I declined, he moved on. "Well, come out for a barbecue."

"It's winter."

"So what?" A challenge in this, a not-so-kind tone. He always tries to lure me out of my cage with food. Instead, I stop eating when I'm troubled by subtext. I've been too thin most of my life.

"Oh, your Uncle Jerry died," he added. "The hospital keeps calling your mother." And he laughed. I could see him leaning his huge belly on the frame of the doorway into the dining-room where they keep the phone, shaking his head—his usual joyless laugh.

"They think she's supposed to deal with it," he said. "He put her down as his next of kin."

"When's the funeral?"

"She's not his next of kin. It's up to Simon."

This obtuseness of my father, his ability to focus on only one small part of anything, has always amazed me. My cousin Simon's strangeness eventually crossed the line into schizophrenia and he has been institutionalized since my Aunt Helen's death. He was older than I, always pale, his speech so soft you might think it was only an echo. Pale blue eyes you would only catch a glimpse of occasionally because he watched his hands as if they were alarming, independent from his will. He had to keep his eye on them. Hard to imagine him capable of anything but that strangely futile vigil.

"Simon's the next of kin," my father repeated.

"That's splitting hairs," I said, shivering at the term.

I can recall in vivid detail the clothes my mother wore when I was a young child. Particularly a white fitted dress gathered in just below her breasts where a shocking line of blood red roses exploding like wounds was appliquéd to her rib-cage, dividing the white encased upper and lower parts of her body. The dress was lined with slippery white, cool against my face when I hid in her dark closet.

She also had tucked away in her closet the clothes my Aunt Helen had made for her. My mother's mysterious wedding dress, which I only saw flat on a hanger, wrapped in plastic. Pearl buttons on the lace over-dress. A satin bodice and pinned to it, a little Juliet cap with the veil springing out.

"She could hide any flaw," my mother told me once. For that reason or some other, Aunt Helen and my uncle had been taken along on her honeymoon. Shielding the wedding dress from light were several other creations, a scarlet satin cocktail dress with spaghetti straps and a black and peach dress with sequined flowers sewn onto the bodice. These were from her trousseau, or later, her days as wife in the Officers Mess, before my father's drinking made outings in such elegant clothes a travesty. She put away the heels with the pointed toes and put on the flat loafers she always wears in the house, her feet clicking up and down the hard-wood floor. She bought a bland succession of earth-toned jackets she wears indoors even in summer.

Of course, clothes are my livelihood. I work out of an office in the basement of what used to be our home. Three of us still live here, but my children have found other homes

to attach themselves to, other people's fridges to raid after
school. They seem to find it sad here. Strange to think that
I fell into this job to be close to them, to prolong my un-
derlife of instinct and nurturing far from the office tower
where I assumed adulthood. But now I see this as a kind of
legacy passed through my mother's family, evidence of how
we are pulled inexplicably back to the past.

I spend days under fluorescent lights with no-one for
company on days without fittings or consultations but four
sizes of dressmaker dummies. Headless, footless, just a swell
of womanly shape from shoulders to breasts and hips. I have
an intimate acquaintance with them now, having eased my
pins from mouth to hand and through their smooth cool
bosoms for years. They've worn the clothes of a hundred
women, women with events to attend, men to excite and
please, needs for concealment, women with their private
pain that seems to flood out when I touch one spot or another. I'm good at my job. I can listen sympathetically and
still keep enough professional distance to reach under a
breast to pin a dart, place my thumb against the warm
groin of a client as I measure for length. Women seem to
feel a need to explain their bodies to me, the scars, the
stretch-marks, the places their flesh has swelled beyond
their wills.

"Did you know that at 37 a woman's eggs suddenly
crash?" one of my regular customers tells me. My age exactly. All day, I walk around feeling transparent and mysteriously bereft, as if I am somehow personally responsible
for something global, perhaps the declining population of
frogs. God knows, with my kids approaching adolescence, I
hardly want my body to spawn again. Plasma generating
magically and spreading out over the highchair, the kitchen
floor, the glass in the windows so you look out at the world
through a film. Dragging my legs through it after a sleepless night. Still, something has changed in women my age.
We've started thinking. Shaken by what we know and all

we sense we still don't know, we suspect how every impulse reverberates with unfinished business.

This morning, my father calls again, but now my uncle's body seems to have replaced grocery shopping as the main attraction. He laughs again and tells me how the hospital called two more times. They don't refer to it as *making arrangements* any more. They talk about claiming the body from the morgue.

"So, is she making the arrangements?" I ask, retreating to the term that still offers them a shred of decency.

"I don't know how they got her name," he answers. "Jerry must have written it down somewhere."

"What did he die of?"

"Oh, nothing really. He was just an old drunk," my father says. My anger burns in my stomach like a flare.

"Dad, I have to go now. I've got work to do."

"When are you going to see your mother?" he asks accusingly. He must be drinking. That is the only time his emotions are this transparent. He is really asking this for himself. My mother seems mildly interested in me. We sit side by side on the couch for brief, pleasant conversations. But my father is attentive in an anxious way. Retiring from the navy must have been like a near-death experience for him and ever since, he's been taken over by grand emotional gestures, constant shopping excursions, loading my fridge with produce that wilts before I even remember it's there.

"I'm going to ask my sister to be an egg donor. I'll try anything at this point," she says above me. Her slim hips are under my hands, encased in pearl-grey jersey.

"It used to be that women my age were stuck. But it's changing every day. After our first three attempts at in vitro failed, we were advised to go to counselling, try to work it through and *Go on with our lives.* Don't you hate it when you're told to go on with your life? That voice from on-high, bossing you around. They might as well be saying: *Go slay the golden calf. Go wander in the desert for 40 days and 40 nights.*"

I laugh along with her. I've been told the same thing too often since my husband, Luke, left. My mother used that exact phrase while she watered her ferns in the blinding afternoon sun.

"Go on with your life. So, you're disappointed. What's new in the universe?" she said. Then, she walked away to the kitchen, clicking in her sensible shoes.

I've moved around to the back of the woman standing before me, but she continues talking, picking up speed as her intensity grows. She tells me eggs may one day be taken like corneas from accident victims. Or harvested from the ovaries of aborted fetuses. She tells me this is the miracle of our age, just as the throwing aside of crutches was a miracle of the past. She talks about being given another chance. A child of a mother who never lived. A woman who is a grandmother before she has even become a mother. It all confuses me. We have enough of our ghosts to put to rest without having them rise up before us in physical form.

But my mother doesn't seem to want another chance. She volunteers no information, doesn't seem to look at me with any curiosity or regret.

When I was about thirteen, I searched every crevice of her life. I searched through her drawers tangled with old girdles, unearthed strange female equipment in a quilted metallic bag, noticed the monthly cycle of her used sanitary pads in the waste-basket in the bathroom still humming with her heat. I was searching for some answer about womanhood and, of course, I was disappointed. Was it revenge that made me cut up with scissors the cocktail dresses and velvet skirts stored in plastic in the back of her closet? I was just making costumes. For years I cut away at her earlier selves. I scissored in half the white dress for the appliquéd roses, which I pressed in a book of fairytales I kept under my bed. I remember now the furtive excitement of taking these things, changing them so they were no longer my mother's, but mine. The only piece of her I would ever really own.

Around that time, I asked her to tell me about my birth. Instead, she told me she had delivered my oldest brother nine months after her wedding, my sister twelve months after that, and me the very next year.

"Women aren't conscious then," she said. "You get stuck doing all the work, that's why they call it labour, then they put you to sleep."

"What do they do to bodies in morgues that are not claimed," I ask the svelte woman stepping up onto my small round platform. She is an internist at the local hospital, and this is the third evening gown I've made for her. This one is dramatic, a blood-red velvet, tapered and flaring out from her thin hips, making her look almost voluptuous. She intends to wear the dress at Carnegie Hall where her nephew is giving his debut performance.

"Are you trying to plan the perfect crime?" she asks me, playful.

"More like the opposite. Maybe I'm trying to prevent the perfect crime. My uncle's body is in the morgue and nobody seems to agree on whose responsibility it is."

"You may not like the answer," she says. "Medical science, for research or teaching. Sometimes private industry makes an arrangement."

"For what?"

"For experiments," she says, raising her arms, deep red and throbbing, as she checks the lift of the skirt. "Look, I don't like telling you this."

"What kind of experiments?"

"Crash test dummies. Car manufacturers."

I'm shocked into silence. I fill my mouth with pins, turn

away from her.

When my father calls again, he doesn't mention my uncle's body. It's been a few days. Something must have happened, but if there had been a ceremony, I would have heard.

"There's a sale on steaks at the IGA," he says.

"We're vegetarian. You know that."

"It's not good for those kids."

I'm suddenly and surprisingly angry, and it's bitter as a taste in my mouth.

"Better for them than booze!" I say. He's silent for a minute. Then he moves on as if I haven't said a thing.

"Your mother's had quite a week," he says. A conspiratorial tone.

"You mean Uncle Jerry's death?"

"They called her day and night. She told them he had a son."

"So, what happened?"

"They must have found Simon. They said a public funeral had been arranged."

I can't imagine my cousin, Simon, arranging anything. *Public funeral* sounds like a euphemism. Probably meaning his body is now in the public domain.

My uncle's ageing unwanted body taken apart in the hands of strangers or sent into mock oblivion over and over in cars crashed against concrete walls. My mother's brother living out other people's tragedies, other people's accidents. He was someone I barely knew. Mostly I remember his and my father's voices late on summer nights as they sat drinking in the back yard when I was a child, their gaiety turned up one notch too loud drifting in my open window. Once when they were visiting, my Aunt Helen, who died of a brain tumour before I was grown, gave me a tiny pair of folding binoculars. "To look into the future," she told me, slipping the little gold chain over my head. I peered through them backwards and saw my mother, too small, far away down a long tunnel, laughing as Aunt Helen put her arm around her shoulders. She was always able to make my mother laugh. After she died, I never again saw my mother incline her head intimately toward anyone.

"I'm ashamed of you both," I tell him. "Where is she?" I demand to know.

He says nothing.

"I want to talk to her, where is she?"

"It's cold out today," he says.

"I'm asking you a straight question." But he's already gone.

The Human Chain

Gerard moves up close behind me as I'm at the sink with bubbling and shimmering pouring down over my hands (God, the light at this time of year), and whispers, "I'll drop Zoe off at the preschool and be back for you. Turn off that fax machine." He leans against me, and the contrast between his solid body suited for work and mine, so flimsily covered by my dressing-gown, leaves me with a film of heat.

"You're out of reach for the morning. Mechanical malfunction," he murmurs.

"And what about you?" I ask, turning and putting my arms around him. He's already been to work and back this morning. Julie rolls her eyes, picks up her book-bag and heads out the door, slipping out of my grasp, just as she always does, when I reach to kiss the top of her head. Zoe sits transfixed before her cereal bowl, watching us with rapt, almost frightened eyes.

"Long story. A fire in a factory in Japan, probably caused by that earthquake a few weeks ago. The price of RAM is going through the roof, so I think we can afford a morning off."

"A windfall, huh?"

"More like earth fall," he says and grins like a child.

Sometimes when we have a rare morning alone, we are raucous together. Today we are shaken by how the mood suddenly changes to tenderness. Something about the light again. How it dazzles gold in the fine curled hairs of his chest.

He feels it too, this enormous good fortune at being physical and alive. As we dress, we speak little. We lock the door behind us, walk hand in hand under the huge maple tree in our front yard and turn onto the street in the direction of the preschool. We approach the elderly couple who pull their ailing golden retriever in a waggon on morning walks. The man lifts the dog from its quilted nest of pink and yellow. He bends over, holding the dog's hips in his hands, supporting the weight as she staggers slowly on the lush grass of our neighbour's front yard. His wife watches intently with a washcloth in her hand, then rushes forward.

Gerard says as we pass them: "If I *ever* act like that, arrange a quick euthanasia."

"No way. You're in this for the long haul," I say.

"Very funny," he says.

Now that we've rounded the corner, we see the steeple of the church that contains the preschool rising needle-like above the vivid blur of green leaves. The church sits empty all week but its basement is a hot-house of children's voices, the chaotic running of feet. The wail of a lone cry echoes in the stairwell as we step through the doors, then the spectacular sight of the preschool opens before us, a festival of red and white. Canada Day flags and posters, balloons and streamers curling red and white everywhere, and children running on a sugar high. The remains of red and white cupcakes litter every surface.

"What's this?" I yell to Irene, the director.

"Canada Day. A little early, but what the heck? They love it," she yells back. "Oh, and sign that card for Terry? She's leaving," she says, smiling at me.

I stand near shelves of toys and board books, holding a large homemade card in my hands. Someone has fastened on red and white helium filled balloons with long strings of ribbon and I feel that the card will drift up out of my hands if I don't hang on. Tendrils of red ribbon ripple below the card, level with my knees. I only vaguely register a small blond baby, barely walking, who tugs the ribbons trailing from the card like umbilical cords. The baby loses his balance, and topples face first into the shelves before I can even think to catch him. He lies on the floor, a sudden cry blossoming along with the blood seeping, then pouring from the split skin on his forehead. I rush to lift him, to soothe him, and his cries heave in my left ear. His rib-cage convulses; he feels as delicate as a baby bird, the little bones all distinct beneath his jumper. I whisper "Shh, Shh," in his ear, holding him close even though I can feel the warmth of his blood spreading on my hands, my arms, on my chest. The warmth spreading from him to me is so intimate it is almost welcome. I place my lips against his temple to comfort him. I taste a warm sticky rust. The swirling mix of children and mothers part before me as I carry him, as if by homing instinct, to the one place I sense he belongs.

She doesn't turn as I approach, and it surprises me that she doesn't have a sixth sense, but she's holding another baby close in age to this one and perhaps these things ebb and flow. She's talking earnestly to Irene.

"Is he yours?" I say once I'm within earshot. The wispy baby in my arms is whimpering now, pitifully, almost hopelessly. She turns to me and gasps. Irene runs from us, fast, returning with a pair of surgical gloves. The mother has quickly put down the child she's holding, has already expertly fished gloves out of her purse and pulled them on her hands with violent snaps. She snatches the baby out of my arms.

"Wash over there," Irene says to me. "*Now!*" So I do, watching the water run pink, then eventually clear. I wash the sleeves of my shirt the best I can, but the stain on my chest will have to wait. I turn back to see Gerard holding Zoe, and talking in close urgent tones to Irene. The mother sits with a can of frozen orange juice wrapped in a cloth and held to the forehead of the baby. Everything has quieted down.

"This shirt has seen better days. It doesn't matter," I say. Zoe reaches out her arms for me.

"I'm kind of wet, sweetie," I tell her. I bend to kiss her on the forehead when Gerard suddenly turns away from me, moving Zoe out of reach. Zoe looks confused, a little angry.

She finds something to complain about. "Mommy, I didn't finish my cupcake." "Where did you leave it? I'll fetch it for you," I say, but Gerard, who is listening, although he seems to be distracted, says: "Don't. You shouldn't touch anything she puts in her mouth."

"He doesn't attend this school," Irene tells Gerard. "He's just visiting with his Mom today. I can't dictate everything," she says almost irritably. I've never heard her voice as anything other than sweetness and light.

The mother looks up at me with a clear gaze. She says, "I'm sorry, but you'll need a shot. Gamma globulin."

"Why?"

"He's a carrier of Hepatitis B. It doesn't hurt. Just a shot in your hip."

Gerard doesn't say anything as we walk into the bright light of the street. The red stain on my chest must be a most magnificent bloom, and we have two blocks to walk home. Even Zoe is quiet.

"That's a dramatic ending to a perfect morning," I say. Gerard doesn't answer.

"How would a child that young pick up Hepatitis?" I say.

"He's from a Romanian orphanage," he says.

"That explains it. I wondered how she could have another child so close in age. It's easily fixed." I reach out and slip my arm through his, surprised at the tension I feel.

"You should ask them about something else," he says. "Ask about AIDS. The baby has it."

All the way here to the hospital, I felt a strange pull in my body, as if I was splitting in two, going in two different directions, and each separated part was less than it was when it was whole. I travelled in the wrong direction away from my home, through unfamiliar neighbourhoods, each seedier than the last, toward this hospital with the old vaulted ceilings and the psychiatric ward, the one with the infectious diseases department. Gerard's idea. He went into his professional mode; looking things up in the phone-book, calling around before telling me, "You need the best possible early assessment. Ask for Dr. Aziz," and he pressed a piece of paper into my hand.

"Hurry," he said, as if it would make a difference.

A woman stopped me on the way here. She knocked on my car window when I was stopped in the part of town where once grand Victorian houses are now reduced to shabbiness. A woman wearing a balding fur coat in late May wandering down the middle of the road. She knocked on the driver's side of each car, came to me, stooping like a hag to see inside. The light didn't change, I was flustered, lowered the automatic window and threw my parking change out. She picked up the change and thanked me in a British accent blurred by her lack of teeth. "Thank you very much, Ma'am." Some reassurance in that strange courtesy, arriving from what I already think of as my other world.

The other half of me is headed in the opposite direction, perhaps, toward the hospital with the pastel birthing-room and friendly nurses. That other half who travelled there twice to give birth to my daughters, is moving away from me fast. I had a sense of this before now though. Giving birth to each of them, I sensed how the skin can stretch and strain and rent suddenly open. I was one, then the pain was so intense, I was nothing, then love flooded me like an anaesthetic, and we were two. I heard Gerard's voice, the voices of the nurses and doctor, hollow and insubstantial, as if they were travelling across water to reach me.

When the labour was coming hard, I was overwhelmed with the revelation that the universe was carried on a current of pain, that I was opening to the pain, sensitive for the first time to the truth. Most of the time our bodies are too dull to perceive much of anything, but *this, this* is real. I never told Gerard. I looked into his eyes and breathed. How important it was to both of us to do well at this. It was some

kind of athletic teamwork, and I never told him how far I
went away from him when he was holding my wrists, gaz-
ing in my eyes, saying "Okay, slow your breathing. I'll
count with you. One, two...slow it down, good." The rent
healed, and I forgot. Skin heals.

My skin, closing like a door, but this time something has
not left. I do not think of this presence as small and infan-
tile and blond as the baby who fell at my feet. I think of it
as all the people sitting around me in this crowded waiting-
room. The woman sitting across from me with a blue plastic
clip on her nose that looks like a clothes-pin, with blood
splattered down the front of her white shirt. She holds a
blood-stained towel on her thick lap. Her eye swelled shut,
red and angry; her open eye is unfocused. She's been split
wide open too.

When I first got here, the nurse at the desk looked at me
suspiciously when I told her I needed to see a doctor. "Is
there something we can do for you?" she asked, her attention pulled away over and over by activity all over the
crowded room. I said what I could never have imagined
myself saying before this moment. "I've been exposed to
Hepatitis and AIDS. A child bled on me."

"It's HIV. Bled on? Where's the child," she said, looking
behind me crossly.

"Another hospital. He just fell. He needed a few
stitches."

"Was he *your* child? Where is he now?" And then I understood that she was worried about the child, not about
me.

"I never saw him before. It was at a nursery school, and
he fell. I picked him up. He was adopted from a Romanian
orphanage."

"What nursery school?" she persisted. Wasn't ready to so
much as look at me until she wrote it down.

"Okay. Any eczema, open wounds? Any blood on your
mucous membranes?" she asked.

"I tasted rust. Maybe some of his blood went in my mouth."

"In your mouth?" she looked up at me with one raised black eyebrow, incredulous. "You'll need a shot. I'll put a call through to Dr. Aziz. You'll have to wait a while," and she turned away, dismissing me.

Yet how kind she is with the young man shrieking at the top of his lungs. "Put it out!" his voice veers into a desperate falsetto. The nurse emerges from behind her counter to bend over him, speaking firmly into his right ear. "Can you hear me? We're going to extinguish the flames. Okay?" she says, and calms him, draws him toward her by never doubting for one minute that the flames are real. She looks up, and smiles faintly at me. I've been here long enough now. I'm starting to belong.

We all sit in orange moulded chairs bolted in lines to the floor. Dark children with rattling coughs climb over the backs, shaking the whole row, occasionally bumping my arms. When I get up to stretch my legs, my orange chair is immediately claimed by a mother who sets her whimpering three-year-old child down. She does not meet my eyes; she doesn't apologize. The girl glances up at me with frightened bleary eyes. Zoe's age, yet she looks like a little wizened old woman. Her skin is purplish brown, as if she is blanched with cold. Her hair is thin, sticking in tufts to her bony skull, so it is obvious she has a fever. She looks away from me, slides down in the chair, lays her head against the hard arm-rest. I find myself thinking that I should take another seat even if this one becomes free again. I should not put my arm on the rest that supports her head, that is filmed with her breath. Would I have bent to pick up this child? I suddenly ache, imagining Zoe, sick and frightened, and nobody reaching for her.

I read a small item in the newspaper a few weeks ago, one of those shocking international stories two inches by two inches on the inner pages of the first section. A little girl drowned in waist-deep water in Holland. Some of the people on the shore tried to reach her by making a human chain, hand to hand, stretching out into the sea, but they couldn't make it long enough because others wouldn't join. The girl was dark-skinned, a refugee, and someone on shore said: "We've got too many. It's not our problem." The photo was small and grainy. It was taken from a high cliff. Dark figures joined at the hands like paper-dolls extending far out, then suddenly ending against a flat horizon of endless water. The girl was already under water, out of reach.

I'm led into a room, stepping around walls of curtains the colour of pale skin, and they move as I walk by them as if they are breathing. My own partition contains only a high plastic bed half covered by a rumpled used sheet. I sit on this bed and wait again. The curtain has been pulled in one rattling screech around me, and soon a man will expertly slip through the slit in the curtains. A woman whimpers softly on the other side of the curtain, maybe only two or three feet away. She waits too. I know that I will hear her story through the curtain, no matter how intimate, how painful it might be, and that she will hear my story. She will hear the shiftings of my body on the bed, the silk slipping from my shoulders.

When the curtain finally opens, it is as if I recognize him. The white of his coat gives his brown skin a dusky cast, as if he has been out in a windstorm in a sandy barren place. His hair is lustrous black under the bright lights. He lifts his brown eyes that have already seen so much to my face. His expression is kind, his movements certain and unhurried. After all the waiting, I'm so glad he's finally here, and I feel a small clenching in my chest. I hold my hand, the one with the wedding ring, out to him. He considers a moment, reaches out and takes it in his own.

ELYSE GASCO was born in Montreal and received an MA in Creative Writing from NYU. Her work has appeared in *Prism, Canadian Fiction Magazine, grain* and *Malahat Review*, and she has won both the 1996 Journey Prize and the 1997 *Prism International* fiction contest. She lives with her husband and daughter in Montreal, where she has completed a collection of stories and is working on a novel.

DENNIS BOCK was born in Belleville. He spent five years writing and teaching in Spain and now lives in Toronto where he is one of the fiction editors for *Blood & Aphorisms*. His first book, *Olympia: A Novel in 12 Stories* will be published by Doubleday in the spring of 1998. His story "Olympia" has been selected to appear in the 1997 *Journey Prize* anthology.

NADINE MCINNIS was born in Belleville, but now lives in Ottawa with her husband and two children. She has published two collections of poetry and one book of literary criticism. Her stories have appeared in *grain, Quarry, Canadian Fiction Magazine* and *Room of One's Own*. A new book of poetry, *Hand to Hand*, will be published this fall.

MAGGIE HELWIG was born in Liverpool, England and grew up in Kingston, Ontario. She edits an occasional litzine and has published one book of essays and five books of poetry, as well as two self-published chapbooks. She has also worked with a variety of peace and human-rights organizations in Canada and England. She now lives in Toronto with her partner Ken Simons and their daughter Simone Helwig.

Previous volumes in this series contained stories by the following writers:

1996: Lewis DeSoto, Murray Logan and Kelley Aitken
1995: Warren Cariou, Marilyn Gear Pilling and François Bonneville
1994: Donald McNeill, Elise Levine and Lisa Moore
1993: Gayla Reid, Hannah Grant and Barbara Parkin
1992: Caroline Adderson, Marilyn Eisenstat and Marina Endicott
1991: Ellen McKeough, Robert Majzels and Patricia Seaman
1990: Peter Stockland, Sara McDonald and Steven Heighton
1989: Brian Burke, Michelle Heinemann and Jean Rysstad
1988: Christopher Fisher, Carol Anne Wien and Rick Hillis
1987: Charles Foran, Patricia Bradbury and Cynthia Holz
1986: Dayv James-French, Lesley Krueger and Rohinton Mistry
1985: Sheila Delany, Frances Itani and Judith Pond
1984: Diane Schoemperlen, Joan Fern Shaw and Michael Rawdon
1983: Sharon Butala, Bonnie Burnard and Sharon Sparling
1982: Barry Dempster, Don Dickinson and Dave Margoshes
1981: Peter Behrens, Linda Svendsen and Ernest Hekkanen
1980: Martin Avery, Isabel Huggan and Mike Mason

Most of these books are still available. Please inquire.